A RUSSIAN DOLL

AND OTHER STORIES

Adolfo Bioy Casares

A RUSSIAN DOLL

AND OTHER STORIES

TRANSLATED BY SUZANNE JILL LEVINE

A NEW DIRECTIONS BOOK

This translation of *Una muñeca rusa,* by Adolfo Bioy Casares, is published by arrangement with Tusquets Editores, S.A., Barcelona.

PUBLISHER'S ACKNOWLEDGMENTS
The stories "The Navigator Returns to His Country" and "A Meeting in Rauch" first appeared in *Bostonia,* the quarterly magazine published by Boston University.

TRANSLATOR'S ACKNOWLEDGMENTS
I would like to thank Diana Thorold for her collaboration on the story "Cato," and the National Endowment for the Humanities for supporting my project of translating the stories of Adolfo Bioy Casares.—SJL

Book design by Sylvia Frezzolini
Manufactured in the United States of America
New Directions Books are printed on acid-free paper.
First published clothbound and as New Directions Paperbook 745 in 1992
Published simultaneously in Canada by Penguin Books Canada Limited

LIBRARY OF CONGRESS CATALOGING-IN-PUBLICATION DATA
Bioy Casares, Adolfo.
[Short stories. English. Selections]
A Russian doll and other stories / Adolfo Bioy Casares ;
translated by Suzanne Jill Levine.
p.   cm.
ISBN: 0–8112–1211–4 —ISBN: 0–8112–1212–2 (pbk.)
1. Bioy Casares, Adolfo—Translations into English.   I. Title.
PQ7797.B535A26   1992   92–10432
863—dc20   CIP

New Directions Books are published for James Laughlin
by New Directions Publishing Corporation,
80 Eighth Avenue, New York 10011

◇◇◇◇◇◇◇◇◇◇◇◇◇◇◇◇◇◇◇◇

Contents

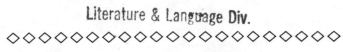

A RUSSIAN DOLL

AND OTHER STORIES

A Russian Doll

My backaches kept me confined for a long time, interrupted only by visits to the doctor and x-ray laboratories. After a year of this I took off for the hot springs, because I remembered Aix-les-Bains. What I mean to say is, its fame for splendid seasons with the most frivolous and elegant people of Europe; and for healing waters that go back to the times before Julius Caesar. In order to change my state of mind and to make my body react I think I needed, even more than the waters, the frivolity.

I flew to Paris, where I spent a little less than a week; then a train took me to Aix-les-Bains. I got off at a small and modest station, which suggested to me the thought: "For good taste, there's nothing like the countries of the Old World. In our America, we are show-offs. Four Aix stations could fit into the new one at Mar del Plata." I'll admit that, upon formulating the last part of this thought, I was pleasantly invaded by patriotic pride.

As I left the station I saw two avenues: one parallel and the other perpendicular to the train tracks. A fisher-

1

man was walking along the parallel avenue, with his rod on his shoulder and a basket. I ignored the offers of a taxi driver and approached the fisherman.

"Could you please show me," I said, "where the Palace Hotel is?"

"Follow me. I'm going there."

"You don't think I should take a taxi?"

"It's not worth it. Follow me."

With some fear that the two suitcases might affect my lower back, I obeyed. We turned down the other avenue, whose first stretch is a steep slope. So as not to think about my back, I asked:

"How was the fishing?"

"Good. Though fishing in a diseased lake isn't—how shall I say—exactly satisfying. We're missing the second part of the program, in which the fisherman makes use of his trophy: he eats what he's fished or gives it to his friends."

"And here you can't do that?"

"In this basket there's a good quantity of *ombles chevaliers*. If you look at them, your mouth will water, but if you eat them, something bad could happen to you. You could get sick, for example. I'm exaggerating, perhaps, but not by much."

"Is that possible?"

"More than possible, probable. The pollution, my dear sir, the pollution. We've arrived."

I was going to say at what, but I realized he was no longer talking about the pollution or the fishing.

"Don't tell me that this is the hotel?" I exclaimed, sincerely perplexed.

"This is it. Why do you ask?"

"No reason."

I took a few steps back and looked at the building: it wasn't small, but neither was it palatial, though at the height of the fourth story I could read, in large letters: Palace Hotel.

In the spacious lobby, with worn-looking chairs, I went over to the reception desk. There, instead of the predictable fellow in a black jacket, a pretty young woman dressed in a gray house smock attended to me.

"Your room is twenty-four," she said. "Follow me, please."

She was lame. In the extremely narrow elevator, with swinging doors that threatened to hit us or trap us, my suitcases, the young woman, and I barely fit. During the slow ascent I could read the instructions for running it and a city ordinance that prohibited minors from using it unaccompanied. We got off at the second floor.

My room was ample, with frayed, yellowing cretonne curtains. In the bathroom the latrine, with its brass bar to hold onto, had deposits on the upper part and a chain. Another brass bar flanked the bidet. The legs of the bathtub ended in claws on white-painted iron spheres.

At one o'clock I went down for lunch. The *maître d'hôtel* came over to me: he was the fisherman I had met upon coming out at the station. I asked him what he recommended. Now in his professional role, he affirmed:

"The duck pâté *à la maison* is justly famous, but I can also offer you some *ombles chevaliers* from the lake."

I said that I preferred red meat. A potato omelette and

then red meat, well done. The food was exquisite, though the portions left something to be desired. A lively, friendly girl named Julie served the table.

With some envy I saw, at the other table, a fellow attended by an even lovelier girl than Julie, as well as by the *maître d'* and the *sommelier*. They all seemed to applaud his words and to rush to meet his desires. I thought: "He must be rich." To confirm this hypothesis there was, beside his table, a bottle of champagne in a silver-plated bucket. I thought: "The gentleman must be very important. Maybe the most powerful industrialist in this region." The portions they served him were considerably larger than mine. This circumstance irritated me and I was about to question Julie. I would have said: "It seems that some are sons and some are stepsons," but since I couldn't find the word in French for "stepsons" I said nothing. When the man stood up and turned around to leave the restaurant, I couldn't believe my eyes. And for good reason. The important man, with his dark curly hair, big movie-star eyes, double-breasted suit, and pointy patent leather shoes, which seemed directly imported from the twenties, was Kid Maceira, my benchmate in primary school. Upon seeing me, he seemed no less surprised than I was myself. He opened his arms, and not caring if he was attracting the attention of the French clientele who were speaking in a discreet murmur, he exclaimed out loud:

"My dear friend! You here! I'll be damned!"

He embraced me. To Julie, who brought my bill, he said that he would sign it later. We went to sit in the chairs in the lobby. As I don't like to talk about my aches and pains, I said that the lumbago was an excuse to come spend a little time out in the great world . . . Maceira interrupted me:

"And who do you meet but the old folks from Welfare. It's too much. The same exact thing happened to me. . . . You know me. I thought: A solid French fortune, nowadays, is the best support an Argentine can get. I came with the crazy dream of finding the most select society and, as I have confidence in myself when it comes to women . . ."

In time he discovered that elegant Aix belonged to former days, before the Second, or perhaps even the First World War.

"Now it has other charms," I said.

"Exactly. But not those we expect."

"Disillusioned?"

"Just like you," he specified, and hugged me once more.

"All jokes aside, you're looking quite prosperous."

"It's not to be believed," he answered, unable to restrain his laughter. "I found what I was looking for."

"A rich woman to marry?"

"Exactly. The story is quite extraordinary. Of course I shouldn't tell it, but brother, with you I have no secrets."

Here's the story that Maceira told me:

He arrived in Aix-les-Bains with the money he earned one lucky day at the Deauville casino. He came with the firm purpose of finding a rich woman. "The great support," he declared.

After the third day of appearing at hotels, eating in restaurants, and listening to the band concert on afternoons in the park, he said to himself: "This is not going anywhere," and he expressed to the hotel owner his intention of leaving the next day.

"That's a pity," she exclaimed, sincerely sorry. "You're going the day before the great ball."

"What ball?"

It was being given by Monsieur Cazalis, "the big industrialist in the region," for his daughter Chantal.

"At the Hotel of the Dukes of Savoie, a veritable palace, in Chambéry."

The lady pronounced with satisfaction the word *palace.*

"Is Chambéry far away?"

"A few kilometers. Very few."

"I don't know why I ask. I'm not invited nor do I have a smoking jacket."

The hotel owner advised that it wasn't worth the trouble to spend money on a smoking jacket for one evening, then to put it away in the closet. She explained:

"Besides, in the stores in Aix, you will not get a custom-made smoking jacket, nor will you find anywhere in France these days a tailor ready to make you a suit for the day after tomorrow. Want me to tell you the secret? Nobody loves his work anymore."

"That's a pity," Maceira murmured, to say something in reply.

"If I were you, I wouldn't discard the possibility of trying on my late husband's jacket," the hotel keeper observed. "Or does that disturb you? Give or take an inch, he more or less resembled you."

The woman took him to her apartment, a veritable

house within the hotel. A very nicely appointed house, which surprised Maceira, whose image of the Palace of Aix was the frayed cretonne curtains in his room and the broken-down chairs in the lobby. "This lame dame really loves herself," he thought. The furniture in the apartment was ancient and quite beautiful, but what attracted my friend's attention was a Russian doll.

"A gift from my father," she said. "I must have been very young or very silly, because my father thought it necessary to explain that it had identical dolls inside, which were smaller. When one breaks, the others are left."

Then she brought in the smoking jacket and said:

"Put it on, while I look for a bow tie that's somewhere around here."

Reluctantly he put it on, but when he looked at himself in the mirror, he exclaimed:

"Not bad."

"As if it had been made to measure," she confirmed, from the doorway.

That Saturday he went to the ball. He had to present an invitation card. He said he had forgotten it. According to him, he got in because the smoking jacket gave him an air of poise.

So as not to attract attention (because he was alone and because he was perhaps the only stranger among all those people) he started up a conversation with an elderly lady. After dancing two or three times with her, he accompanied her to the buffet. They raised champagne glasses in a toast, when a blonde and very beautiful girl ("Perhaps," he thought, "one of those strong, golden Belgian girls I like so much") intervened and said to him:

"Since you haven't asked me to dance, I'll ask you."

She laughed with irresistible joy. As they danced, she asked him not to get angry ("As if I could have gotten angry") and added that upon seeing him monopolized "by that lady" she considered it her duty to rescue him. She then took him over to a table where she had friends and introduced them. Maceira quickly thought: "When I have to give my name, they'll find me out." By which he meant: "They'll find out I'm an intruder." He didn't have to give his name and suspected that she wanted to make him believe that she knew him, or perhaps make the others believe . . . He explained to me:

"A woman who has her eye on you, doesn't want to find reasons to let you go."

"Lucky man," I said.

"More than you can imagine."

"You're not going to tell me that she was the industrialist's daughter?"

"Precisely."

He then admitted that he was so eager to flatter her that he almost made the wrong move. It seems he told her:

"I take my hat off to your father. This ball is the gesture of a great man."

Chantal fixed a worried look on him, as if she wanted to figure out what he was thinking, until she started laughing in that joyous way that was so her.

"Wise guy!" she exclaimed. "You fooled me! I thought you were serious! Rest assured that my father can give all the parties in the world but he won't buy me."

She immediately explained, as if impelled by an obsession, that the ecological group to which she and Benjamin Languellerie belonged had undertaken a campaign against her father's company, whose factory was contaminating Lake Bourget.

Maceira did not disregard the name of Benjamin Languellerie. He instantly suspected that the man was a rival. A reassuring explanation immediately followed: Languellerie, a friend and a contemporary of her father, was a kind of old uncle to Chantal. He knew her since she was a little girl and, despite their disparate ages, the friendship between them had never floundered. There was, however, a change: after a number of years (the first fifteen or sixteen years of the young girl's life), Languellerie went from protector to follower. He had sheltered her from her father's severity and then he followed her through a series of passing obsessions, such as psychoanalysis, baking, and ballet, right up to the last one, ecology. The fact that he affiliated himself with the ecology group proved that if he had to choose between father and daughter, he chose the daughter. Cazalis could not forgive him that affiliation, because the ecology group and the war on his factory were at that time one and the same. The factory workers printed pamphlets and scribbled rough graffiti calling Languellerie a Judas; Mr. Cazalis, in some communication to his daughter, did likewise.

Maceira was about to ask Chantal if her father was around so that she could point him out—"to know who my father-in-law was"—when he reflected that he should repress his curiosity: if the girl found out he didn't know Mr. Cazalis, she could very well deduce that he had not been invited by him and that he was an intruder. "Who knows," he said to himself, "if in one fell swoop I wouldn't lose all that I'm gaining."

The night of the ball was followed by daily encounters between Chantal and Maceira, encounters that very soon became passionate. The love she expressed to him in words and deeds secretly convinced Maceira, "an incredulous old fox," that they were on their way to marriage. "What more could I want," he said to himself. "She's perfect and I enjoy life with her." He assured me:

"I never heard her say anything stupid. Perhaps the only stupidity I could pin on her was the ecology thing. And even that I'm not convinced was stupid. All I'd say here is that to protect this poor earth of ours I wouldn't move a finger. On the other hand, Chantal's attitude proved to me her decency. It was not to be believed: she was resolved to wage war against her own interests. Against our interests. If it had been up to me I wouldn't have given up one cent of Monsieur Cazalis's millions, but there's so much that even if the factory were closed down, Chantal and I could still live in the lap of luxury and without the slightest care for the rest of our lives. I don't know if I'm making myself clear: if she didn't care about reducing her inheritance, I didn't either, within certain reasonable limitations."

Then began a period that Maceira would not forget easily. Even though he slept every night in his hotel in Aix, most of the time he spent with Chantal, in Chambéry, or on excursions in the Savoie, one of the most beautiful regions of France. They went to Annecy, to La Charmette, to Belley, to Collonge where there's a castle, to Chamonix, to Megève. After marking on a map of the region the cities and villages where they had been, Chantal asserted:

"To know one's province well, there's no better way than having a love affair with a foreigner."

She would also add comments such as: "We still haven't made love in Evian."

Within Chantal's group Maceira's situation was acknowledged and respected. He would often say to himself: "I'm in luck." Now and then only one little worry would jolt him: how long would his money last. Chantal, in effect, did not have the habit of paying (typical in some rich women and always offensive to masculine pride). Between the enviable excitement of his afternoons and the well-earned sleep of his nights, Maceira had little time left to brood. Besides, even though the grand total of the inn and restaurant bills could alarm him, each one filled him with pride.

Of course, they did not spend together the hours Chantal dedicated to the ecology group; but afterward the girl would openly recount to him every vicissitude of the campaign against the paternal factory. On one occasion she commented that activists from the workers' union were sending threatening letters.

"To whom?" asked Maceira.

"To me, of course. And to poor uncle Benjamin, as I call Languellerie."

Although there was no lack of justified alarm, over the

threats of the letters as much as over the accumulation of
expenses, that era was a happy one. Maceira was even a
little surprised by the triumphant development of his
life.

"As you can well understand, I couldn't quite accept
it."

"I don't understand."

"Out of superstition, of course. I am more superstitious than an artist and I thought that admitting my
lucky star would bring me bad luck. That I was lucky,
there is no doubt," he stated, apparently forgetting his
superstitious code. "Or do you think I'm exaggerating?
Loved by a woman who was as beautiful as she was rich,
always ready to give me proof of her love and to tell, to
whomever wished to listen to her, her plans for our
marriage . . . My only fear, of course, was that the
wedding wouldn't happen in time. I mean, before I ran
out of francs. The truth is that it was purely fate that had
brought me this woman who was splendid in every
sense. If I was told what I spent alone on gas for Chantal's Delahaye, I'd drop dead."

There was no lack of compensations. The girl lent him
her car so that at night he could return to his hotel. No
matter how late it was, at the wheel of that twelve-
cylinder Delahaye, he was in no rush, because he saw
himself as "destiny's favorite" and he wanted to con-
sciously enjoy the situation.

When he stopped to reflect he realized that the pleasant moments he was living would either carry him fatally
to victory, that is, marriage, or to the lack of funds and

withdrawal in defeat: whichever came first. An unforeseen event changed everything.

They had spent the afternoon at an inn at Saint Albin (or perhaps some other town with a similar name). As the sun was setting they went over to the window, to look at the lake before leaving.

"It's not as large as the one at Aix or Annecy, but I like it more," said Chantal. "Perhaps because it's unspoiled."

Maceira agreed, though he had no opinion about the matter. "It must be very beautiful," he said to himself, "but it seems less cheerful than the others." Flanked by a steep mountain, at dusk it was rapidly fading into darkness.

"When we're together I forget everything. I didn't tell you that we're winning."

Maceira asked:

"Winning what?"

Chantal explained that not only would they be taking new water samples from different areas of Lake Bourget, but the following day a zoologist and a botanist, recommended by the ecology group, would go down to the bed of the lake, with Monsieur Cazalis himself, to gather specimens of the fauna and flora. Chantal commented:

"The bad part is that my father has lots of money."

"What's bad about that?"

"For money people give up their convictions," the girl stated, in the grave tone she would use to talk about ecology. "As honest as our zoologist and our botanist may be . . ."

"Your father can buy them?"

"Why not? To be completely sure I'd have to go down, or Benjamin. My father refuses to let me go down. Not because he loves me, but because he thinks that he and I shouldn't run the same risk at the same time. If both of us die, the factory will pass into other hands, an idea he cannot accept."

"And he doesn't accept Benjamin because he's furious at him?"

"The one who's against it is me. Benjamin is too old. A few grains of salt can give him high blood pressure. If something happens to him down there and he has to come up quickly, the poor man will explode."

Confident of the probability that she wouldn't let him go down, Maceira offered his services. His fiancée reacted with gratitude.

"I don't want to force you," he said. "Maybe you don't trust me."

"How could I not trust you!"

"If all men have a price . . ."

"Of that I am sure, but I know that there are exceptions and I love you."

He was left with the satisfaction that Chantal trusted him. In any case, she hugged and kissed him more affectionately than ever. They ordered champagne.

"To your courage," the girl toasted.

"To our love."

"To our love and to ecology."

She indulged him so much that night that after leaving Chantal in Chambéry he returned to Aix in a kind of rapture, without remembering his thankless task for the next day. At the precise moment he entered his room, in the hotel, the rapture disappeared. One might say that fear was awaiting him.

All through the night the urge to run away over- whelmed him in fits and outbursts. A little before three in the morning he had an outburst that was more con- vincing than the previous ones; he got up from bed and began to pack his suitcases. It was curious: as he packed, his anguish disappeared. What didn't let him calm down completely was the excitement of knowing he was about to be saved. He had already grabbed his two suitcases, when he asked himself: "Do I want to give up my mar- riage with Chantal Cazalis?" No, he didn't want to. He next argued that diving to the bed of the lake, an irre- futable proof of loyalty and courage, would give him the authority to fix the date of the wedding and to avoid the risk of being left without funds and seeing himself obliged to undertake an awkward retreat.

He thought: "In relationships with rich women, if the man gets careless, the woman becomes the man. Proof of manly courage will perhaps set things right."

Throughout his night of insomnia, fear reappeared many times and many times he repressed it. Toward dawn he reflected that if Monsieur Cazalis, a botanist, and a zoologist were willing to descend, the danger couldn't be that great. With these tranquilizing thoughts he managed to sleep. When he awoke he said: "How- ever, Chantal doesn't want Languellerie to go down, nor does Cazalis want his daughter to go down, who's stronger than a horse." This expression was not proof that in his heart of hearts he didn't love Chantal. It proved what we all know: fear makes us angry.

The alarm clock went off at six. Maceira looked out the window: it was still night; it was raining; gusts of wind shook the treetops. "With weather like this they'll probably suspend the experiment. I hope so."

He bathed, combed his hair with brilliantine, got dressed. They took a while to serve him breakfast. It wasn't brought by the same woman as always, but rather by a fellow who usually worked as a porter in the hotel.

"I have something else," the man announced; he rapidly left the room and returned with a voluminous package. "It was left at the front desk. It's for you."

As soon as the porter left, Maceira opened the package and found a diving suit with its frogman fins and mask. "The confirmation that the plan is on," he said with a faltering voice. "Of course if the bad weather keeps up . . . No, I don't want to get my hopes up." As if to confirm his statement, he put on the diving suit. He went over to the mirror. "I prefer the smoking jacket," he murmured and began his breakfast. The coffee was lukewarm. "What does it matter. Though it's not my fault, I'm going to arrive after seven and maybe Cazalis doesn't like to wait. But I shouldn't get my hopes up." When he dunked his croissant in the bowl of coffee with steamed milk, he had a thought that seemed ridiculous to him but which made his eyes water. "Maybe my last croissant," he said to himself. He looked at it tenderly.

When he turned in his key, Felicitas—the hotel owner's name—commented in a joking tone:

"What an hour to go to a masked ball."

"Keep my secret," Maceira replied. "In a little while I'm going down to the bottom of the lake, to gather evidence of contamination."

The poor cripple looked frightened:

"Why are you doing it? Are they paying you well?"

"Nothing."

"You want to know what I think? I wouldn't go down if I were you. You don't have any idea how deep our dear lake is. Hundreds and hundreds of meters. Don't go down; but if you insist upon this stupid project, remember what I'm telling you: go down and come up slowly. Remember: you hurry and your head will explode."

The meeting place was the restaurant in the so-called Grand Port. When he arrived, the only person in sight was a sailor with a pipe, blue jacket, and cap with a red tassel. "Too typical to be a lake sailor," thought Maceira. By the way he was smoking, he didn't seem happy. He approached Maceira and said:

"You're in the excursion? Congratulations. Whoever goes out sailing on a day like today is not all well up here," he touched his forehead and, upon seeing that Maceira did not respond immediately, he warned him: "If we're wrecked, I'll charge you for the boat."

"That would be fine and dandy. I'm coming along out of obligation and you're making me responsible."

"Of course I'm making you responsible. You yourself must realize that the lake is very rough. There is no visibility."

"Tell all that to Cazalis. He organized the excursion."

"It's not going to be an excursion. When the lake gets rough, it's worse than the sea. Remember the poet's sweetheart? She was drowned in the middle of the lake, on a day like today."

"Talk to Cazalis."

"Of course I'm going to talk. To go out in such weather, they're going to have to pay me a double fee."

"What I don't understand is why, if the factory is on the other end, we're embarking here. It's good for me since I live in Aix."

"You live in Aix? A point in your favor. But even though it's good for you, do you realize what it is to go from one end of the lake to another in this weather? If we don't capsize on the way there, we'll capsize on the return."

Maceira repeated that he didn't understand why Cazalis decided to set out from Aix and added:

"I don't think it was my comfort he had in mind."

"He was thinking of the workers. He doesn't want them to find out."

The sailor made him see that if the port of departure had been near Chambéry, some information "would have filtered out" and the workers wouldn't have calmly allowed them to investigate whether or not there were good reasons to close the factory where they earn their bread.

Maceira said to himself that if Cazalis and the experts didn't show up in ten minutes, he would return to the hotel, with the clear conscience of having done his duty. "When they're late, it's because they couldn't get here earlier; when I'm late, it's because I'm South American. I'll bet that upon seeing how the weather is, Cazalis left the excursion for a better occasion."

Three gentlemen in diving suits appeared, walking in a ridiculous way. One of them was heavyset, with a big blond mustache and the air of a Viking, or rather Norman conqueror; another one, a little man, moved so slowly that Maceira wondered if he were ill, or mentally solving a problem, or drugged; the third one, with a rather dark complexion, seemed angry or nervous. Maceira hurried to greet the one who looked like a conqueror. He said:

"Nice to meet you, Monsieur Cazalis."

"Here is Monsieur Cazalis," the Norman replied, indicating the little man.

"I, on the other hand, can make no mistake: you are Maceira."

This said, the little man stared at him without blinking an eye; then he shook his head, with resignation. He did not shake his hand.

"I'm Le Boeuf," said the one who looked Norman.

"I think I've heard your name," Maceira commented.

"You've probably seen it on coal-tar dye bottles. The pride of my family. Allow me to introduce you to the zoologist Koren."

After gathering his courage, Maceira warned Cazalis:

"The sailor says it isn't wise to go out on the lake in this bad weather."

"If you're afraid, don't come."

The sailor took Cazalis aside and, after whispering, raised his voice to say:

"Everybody on board."

"The bad weather is an excellent excuse to raise the price," Cazalis observed, with surprisingly good humor; then, looking at Maceira, he added: "You can be sure that the experiment does not appeal to me one bit, but I said that today I'd carry it out successfully, and I'm a man of my word."

"Nobody else is coming?" asked the sailor.

"Nobody else," Cazalis answered. "We're already too many."

"The first piece of truth you've said," declared the sailor. "The lake is rough and we've got a big load."

Maceira whispered to Cazalis:

"If you want, I'll stay behind."

"Since you represent the other side, they'll say I arranged it to leave you out," Cazalis answered, and, with a smile, he added ironically:

"No, thinking it over carefully, I will not allow that because of us you are deprived of this pleasure trip."

When they all got in, the edges of the boat were almost at water level.

"Gentlemen," said the sailor. "You will be able to see that there is a little can at the disposal of each passenger. Please use it. You have to take out the water that comes in, especially if you don't want to sink. It is no short trip to the other side of the lake."

"With weather like this," Maceira thought, "how does the sailor know we're going toward the most advantageous point? What's most probable is that he no longer knows where we are."

The wind did not die down; rather it was getting stronger, and consequently the navigation, hazardous to begin with, was becoming a little less than impossible. Despite everything the sailor did not stop rowing. At some moment Maceira, despairing of the utility of any effort, tried to rest for a second from his task with the can. The sailor immediately reprimanded him:

"Hey you! Don't play the fool! Keep bailing out that water, if you don't want us all to drown!"

Maceira reflected: "This man is trying to convince us that he's a wizard at direction. In reality he's a scoundrel. He doesn't know where we are nor where we're going. When he gets tired, he's going to say: 'It's here,' and like idiots we're going to believe him." To do anything to cut short that endless first part of the excursion, he would have gladly said what they were surely all thinking. "Let's stop for once and for all. . . . One point of the lake is as good as the next." He restrained himself for fear that Cazalis would repeat his words to Chantal.

"We've arrived," announced the sailor.

"Hurrah," exclaimed the botanist.

"Too bad we have to go down," said the zoologist.

"That's true. I had forgotten . . ." the botanist replied cheerlessly.

"Gentlemen, let's get this over with. I'll go down first," Cazalis announced.

"Me last," Maceira hurried to say.

"Sailor: don't get distracted. If we want to come up, we'll pull on the rope; two pulls, if we want to come up quickly."

"You'd do better not to come up quickly," the sailor commented indifferently.

The descent was long, according to Maceira, and at least for him very alarming. Suddenly he heard sounds, without knowing from where, that reminded him of water flowing out of a drainpipe. Two or three times, "merely because of nerves," he was about to pull on the rope. He wondered if at some moment he would reach the bottom and if the lake had a bottom.

He finally felt under his feet a bed of clay and leaves. He looked ahead and could see the rest of the group advancing toward the mouth, in the shape of an arch, of a vegetal tunnel, dark in the center and formed by enormous blue plants with fleshy leaves, intertwining above. "If they're going in there they're very brave," thought Maceira. That thing was like a lion's den: a dark surface, a veritable lion's den, surrounded by plants that looked like snakes. Not snakes: boas. Not to be surpassed by the others he tried to move ahead, but distrust must have paralyzed him, because he didn't take a single step. When he told me this, Maceira said: "People can say what they want about Kid Maceira, but not that he's a coward. Now I want to explain: one thing is everyday life and another is to be at the bottom of Lake Bourget."

When he was finally going to make a move, two yellowish blue lights appeared in the upper half of the mouth of the tunnel. He thought they were fog headlights. Oval-shaped lights, like the eyes of an enormous cat. He suddenly noticed, not without concern, that the lights moved, advanced, very slowly. He had time to imagine something incredible: a truck "there at the bottom of the lake?" which was suddenly going to speed up and run him over. He remained ready and, at the right

moment, would jump to one side and pull twice on the rope. He had time, also, to see how a very long animal slid out of the tunnel, an enormous blue caterpillar that diligently, but without any hurry, devoured, one by one, Monsieur Cazalis, the zoologist, the botanist. Perhaps because the events occurred in silence they left him a memory that didn't seem quite real. This did not prevent him from getting scared, as a frantic series of pulls on the rope proved. They were so frantic that the sailor got alarmed. At least he reacted as if he were alarmed or irritated: forgetting all precaution, he pulled up Maceira as quickly as he could. To absolve himself of blame he would be able to contend that if he had been less expeditious, Maceira would not have escaped the caterpillar. He reached the surface ill, his face covered with bruises from being banged against the keel of the boat. He didn't speak, he didn't answer questions. He moaned, put his hands to his head.

At the Public Health Clinic in Chambéry he received immediate care, but they quickly sent him to the hospital in Aix, where there was a decompression chamber.

After several days, he got better.

"In all the time I've been in this hospital, nobody has come to see me?" he asked the nurse.

She was blonde, young, and had rings under her eyes. Her eyes expressed fatigue or concern.

"I don't know. We'll have to ask at the front desk."

"And telephone calls?"

"Are you anxiously waiting for a call? I don't know why you ask, if you're not going to tell me . . . There's really no reason why you should hide anything from your nurse. While we have you here you're affectionate, but as soon as you set foot on the street you'll forget me. Very sad."

He asked the night nurse—she was voluminous and maternal—the same questions.

"You'll have to talk to Larquier."

"Who's Larquier?"

"The one who left awhile ago, the day nurse. At night we don't accept visitors and the calls are usually emergencies. However, it seems to me that during the first nights a lady called."

"Chantal Cazalis?"

"Of course. I'll confirm it for you later. I have the call written down."

"Can I now receive visitors?"

"You can receive whomever you want."

The morning of the next day he said to Nurse Larquier:

"If a blonde young lady appears, let her in."

In the afternoon Maceira received his first visitor, a journalist, who asked him:

"Are you better? Do you think you could answer a few questions? I don't want to tire you out."

"Ask," Maceira replied.

He reflected: "I'd better think quickly. Should I or shouldn't I tell what happened at the bottom of the lake? If I say that I didn't see anything and that I pulled on the rope because I felt ill, what happened down there will remain a mystery, but I won't have given a single argument in favor of closing the factory, and when we marry and receive all of Monsieur Cazalis's fortune, minus the

taxes, I will have more than enough reasons to congratulate myself, but—what the hell!—though it be for once
in my life I want to be loyal to the woman that destiny
has placed beside me. If what I say now will cause the
closing of the factory and one day I'll regret not having
lied, it doesn't matter; for once I want to be loyal,
blindly loyal."

"The first question," said the journalist, "is: What did
you see at the bottom of the lake? What happened there,
exactly?"

Maceira tried to be truthful, not to leave anything out,
except his personal reactions. He wanted to be objective.

The journalist listened to him in silence. Then he
begged him to talk more about the caterpillar.

"Was it very big? Big for a caterpillar?"

"A gigantic animal."

"What diameter?"

"Four meters at least. The last time I saw Le Boeuf, a
man approximately six feet tall, he was standing in the
open mouth of the caterpillar."

After several questions of little importance, when he
was already on his way out, the journalist passed on to
personal questions, like: "Have there been any cases of
madness in your family?" "Were you ever confined in a
mental hospital?"

Finally the journalist left. Maceira asked the nurse if
Mademoiselle Chantal Cazalis had come to visit him or
had asked for him. He was told no.

"I'm surprised she hasn't come."

"It's the blonde you were expecting? I'm going to tell
them to let her in."

The next day Larquier announced that the young blonde had arrived. Maceira asked her to tidy up the room a bit, and got up to wash himself, comb his hair, and make sure in the mirror that his pajamas were presentable. He admired how precisely and quickly the nurse fixed the bed, with a juggler's dexterity; after a brief play of hands, the sheets and blankets seemed new.

A blonde, unknown girl came into his room.

"I'm representing the personnel at the factory," she said. "I'm pleased that you've received me. Now you won't be able to state that we didn't let you know."

She was one of those blondes, usually Belgian, that he liked so much.

"I don't understand," he assured her.

"It doesn't matter. I think there are more serious issues that you don't understand either."

"What issues?"

"You know what I'm talking about. Did you or did you not go down to the bottom of the lake as a representative of the ecology group that intends to close the factory? . . ."

"If I hadn't gone down I wouldn't be here. Besides, the owner of the factory went down."

"The truth is I thought I'd find you healthy and in good shape. If you could get up for a moment to come to the window, you'd see something interesting."

The girl's tone was hostile. Maceira thought: "I should tell her that I can get up, but out of a lack of curiosity I'm not going to." . . . However, his curiosity was greater than his good judgment. He got up, went to the window, looked at the street and the houses on the other side.

"I don't see anything extraordinary," he declared.

"You don't see a man, there, on the left? Now, please, look to the right. Do you see the other one?"

"So what about them?"

"They're pickets. When you go out, they'll be there to receive you. They're from the labor union."

"Are they there to attack me? Have you all gone crazy?"

"You have nothing to fear if you don't continue your campaign and if you don't make compromising statements."

"What do you call compromising statements?"

"You'll find out when you leave this building."

"You've all gone crazy."

"You're mad because you're afraid they'll hurt you," the girl replied and continued, now shouting: "Do you care if you harm the five hundred people who could lose their jobs overnight because of you? Answer that!"

Nurses, male and female, entered the room in an alarmed state.

"What's going on here?"

"Nothing," Maceira assured them.

"A lover's quarrel?" Larquier asked in a mocking tone.

Another nurse questioned the girl:

"Weren't you ever told it was bad manners to shout in a hospital? I'm telling you now."

"You're right and I'm sorry."

"I can assure you that your feeling sorry matters little to me. This visit is over."

Minutes later, when Larquier brought him some pills, Maceira said:

"Do you know why that blonde came? To threaten me."

"How horrible!" Larquier exclaimed sadly. "The blonde seemed so serious it didn't occur to me she had bad intentions. I should tell you that I knew perfectly well she wasn't Mademoiselle Cazalis, but I let her come in, so that you would be disappointed. I'm a fool and you're not going to forgive me. We should call the police."

"Okay," Maceira answered. "But not from the telephone on this floor. There must be a telephone booth somewhere in the hospital."

"Yes, more than one, on the first floor."

Larquier agreed with him: anybody could hear him if he spoke from the telephone on the floor. She added that it was very important for him to make that call and promised to talk to the doctor on duty, to get permission for him to go downstairs.

The doctor said that he found Monsieur Maceira much improved and that it was time for him to begin to circulate in the corridors. He wasn't opposed to his going downstairs to the telephone booths properly accompanied by the nurse.

At no moment did Maceira have the intention of calling the police. He called Chantal's house. They told him there:

"The young lady left for Paris because of legal problems; she was disappointed not to have seen you, but the police warned her not to go to the hospital, because there were pickets of activists on guard; from the nurses she received good news about Monsieur Maceira's health."

He then looked in the directory for the number of the newspaper and spoke with the journalist. The latter, excusing himself, announced to him that the article would come out the next day. When Maceira asked if there wouldn't be any possibility of his giving a quick look at his statements, the journalist promised him:

"If they confirm that it's coming out tomorrow, I'll take it to you this afternoon. Okay? Perfect!"

As he left the booth he noticed a certain animation in the eyes of the nurse, who said:

"I want you to tell me. I'm dying of curiosity."

"For now there's no need to talk about the matter. We could pay very dearly for it. I promise, I cross my heart, that you'll be the first to know."

He thought that he was living intense hours. The moments of satisfaction and those of anxiety alternated vertiginously. Whether one liked it or not, the article, the blonde's threats, had turned him into one of the most important patients in the hospital.

That afternoon the journalist did not bring the article to him. The next morning nurse Larquier entered his room waving the paper in her hand.

"Look what I'm bringing you. It occupies a whole page. You'll have to celebrate it with champagne; but not with the blonde. With us."

Nervously Maceira glanced over his statements. Feeling a cold sensation in his veins, he thought: "Now I'm really in trouble." He lamented having gone against his own interests, and he came to ask himself if he shouldn't admit to them that they were right, that he had acted foolishly, prejudicing his own case, because he was going to marry Chantal. He would promise them to fight, from now on, to avoid the closing of the factory, and he would make them see that his interests coincided completely with theirs. He then reflected: "It's useless. Those people are hard. They don't forgive."

In reality the interview occupied less than a half page; in a square in the center, though. It read: "A blue caterpillar, with cat eyes. Survivor denounces." He continued reading:

Journalist: How deep did you all go down?

Monsieur Maceira: At least a hundred meters . . . I say this because of how long it took us to get to the bottom.

Journalist's note: Well-informed sources state that the depth reached could not have exceeded twenty-five or thirty meters.

Journalist: What color was the caterpillar?

M. Maceira: Blue. Down there everything is blue.

Journalist: In your opinion, what does the caterpillar feed on?

M. Maceira: On the refuse from the factory. It seems obvious.

Journalist: Why?

M. Maceira: We went down to find out if there was evidence of pollution. We found the most extraordinary evidence: a caterpillar three or four meters in diameter.

In lakes free of pollution nobody has found such a monster.

Journalist: Before people spoke of pollution, a monster appeared in a lake in Scotland, but let's leave that aside. What happened to those who accompanied you in the dive?

M. Maceira: They were devoured by the caterpillar.

Journalist: Didn't you say that this monster fed only on the refuse from the factory?

M. Maceira: I don't think that before Cazalis and the two experts other gentlemen had served as nourishment.

Journalist's note: Upon hearing this display of M. Maceira's strange sense of humor, I brought the interview to a close.

The displeasure that the reading of the newspaper provoked in him was augmented by the news that the doctor gave him.

"Before you know it you will be leaving our hospital. Congratulations."

Maceira thought that he should overcome his fear and be happy that very soon he would see Chantal. He called her on the telephone to give her the news. The secretary told him that Mademoiselle Chantal was still in Paris. Maceira thought: "My place is in Paris, beside the woman I love and far from the factory activists."

On what would be his last night at the hospital, Nurse Larquier suggested that he go down to the conciergerie, to play cards with the "man in the booth" (the telephone operator) and the doorman. After two or three rounds, Larquier said that she would go to the kitchen to prepare coffee for everyone and, especially, for her little patient, to keep him from catching cold on such an intemperate night. Despite her pretense to express joy, in the way she looked at him Larquier seemed anxious, perhaps desperate. Maceira reflected that some men—among whom he included himself, of course—seduced women without even trying. The telephone operator talked about the pickets. Accompanied by the doorman, Maceira approached the street door. The doorman opened it a crack and looked. Maceira asked:

"Are they still there?"

"I don't see them," replied the doorman. "You look."

As soon as he stuck out his head, someone on the outside held him down, picked him up, wrapped him in something thick and hairy, which turned out to be a blanket, and put him in a vehicle.

"Don't move, don't get up, don't talk," a woman's voice whispered—which he didn't immediately recognize because he was confused and a little scared.

Despite his bewilderment he reflected that Nurse Larquier had betrayed him miserably . . . "I'm a stupid jerk," he thought. "With women you should never let down your guard."

At first they went at a great speed, braking abruptly and squeaking the tires around curves. Then the pace became calmer. A voice he recognized as that of the *maître d'* of the restaurant at the Palace Hotel asked:

"Are you sure they're not following us?"

"Completely," the feminine voice answered, which Maceira now recognized as Felicitas', the hotel owner. "Let's go home, Julio."

"Can I sit up?" Maceira asked.

"Not until we enter the hotel garage. I'll let you know when."

They took off the blanket. Felicitas begged him to forgive them for the way they had proceeded, but said that after his statements to the newspaper the factory workers were furious.

"You'll spend a few days hiding in the hotel. The important thing is that they not know where to find you. When they get tired of picketing in Aix-les-Bains, they'll return to Chambéry and you'll be able to do what you want."

Maceira didn't know if he should be happy about hiding or regretting the postponement of seeing Chantal.

During the first days he was overwhelmed by anxiety. He kept deciding to call Chantal, but also continuously thought that he shouldn't commit such an imprudence. Finally he called. They told him that Chantal had not returned from Paris. The next day he called again. When he asked for Chantal, they put him in touch with Languellerie, who said to him:

"I would like to see you."

"You don't know how happy I am that you're on the phone. I've already lost track of the number of times I called Chantal."

"I know, I know. I have a message for you from her. I'm supposed to give it to you personally."

"What should I do?" thought Maceira. "Chantal's friend and protector wouldn't betray me."

"Are you sure the line isn't being tapped?"

"Completely sure."

"I'm in the Palace Hotel in Aix."

"I'll visit you this very evening."

"Don't say you're coming to see me and make sure they're not following you."

He spent an agitated afternoon. When he announced to Felicitas that Languellerie would visit him, the woman got angry. She said:

"You're not worth the trouble we took to rescue you."

Maceira attempted explanations ("Languellerie is a faithful friend, we can trust him completely," et cetera), but the cripple lost all patience and left, banging the door.

Maceira received Languellerie with a show of affection. He explained: "I saw in him an ally." The old man, on the other hand, greeted him inexpressively and said:

"I won't hide the fact that your statements to the newspapers caused a deplorable impression."

"I know perfectly well. The activists . . ."

"I'm not speaking about the activists," Languellerie clarified. "I'm speaking about us. About Chantal and myself. Chantal has inherited from her father the management of the factory and you, an intimate friend in people's opinion, without consulting anybody, come out with inconvenient, or more to the point, inopportune statements."

"I made them out of loyalty to Chantal. I thought . . ."

"What you thought is of no interest to us. Before speaking, didn't you stop to think that Chantal's situation had undergone a change? From being a girl without any responsibility whatsoever, who as a private citizen could allow herself the least conventional opinions, moved on to be the head of an empire and the sole owner of a factory where five hundred workers are employed. I'm not sure I'm making myself clear: In this new situation can Chantal look with approval upon someone who's fighting to close down her factory?"

"I understand," said Maceira, angrily.

"If you understand," replied Languellerie, "I don't know why you're speaking in that tone. The closing of the factory would signify unemployment for five hundred people and poverty for two or three times that number. Accept the advice of an old friend: Stay calm, don't open your mouth, wait for people to forget and for Chantal to forgive. I promise to mediate for you."

There was a silence, as if Maceira assumed the story he had told me was finished. I asked:

"Did Languellerie keep his word?"

"He married Chantal."

"I don't believe you!"

"Believe me. For some time I was quite bitter. It's amazing how long it took me to discover that Felicitas had a lively inclination toward me. Though lame, she's fairly pretty and perhaps in the long run easier to get along with than the other one. With women, who can be sure? Who can foresee how they will turn out? I admit that between the two fortunes there is no comparison, but the most acclaimed hotel in a French city, famous for its waters, is definitely a great support. On the other hand, as we well know, any industry can produce wealth today and hunger tomorrow."

"Are you going to marry Felicitas?"

"We're already married, old man. Mission accomplished. You're speaking to the very owner of the Palace Hotel."

A Meeting in Rauch

Thursday morning, at eight o'clock sharp, I was to appear at the ranch of Don Juan Pees in the district of Pardo, to conclude a cattle sale, the first important transaction I was to bring to the auction house in the city of Rauch where I worked. I had gotten this job in December 1929, and if I was still at it a year later, perhaps I owed it to the esteem the members of the firm professed for my elders.

At breakfast on Wednesday, we spoke about the following day's trip. My mother insisted that I couldn't miss the appointment, even though Thursday was Christmas. To avoid any excuse to postpone it, my father lent me the automobile, a double phaeton Nash, "his favorite child" as we said at home. They certainly did not want me to lose the business, on account of the commission, a considerable sum, and because if I lost it I could very well be out of a job. The crisis was severe; people were already talking about the unemployed. Apart from all that, perhaps my parents thought that because of such strokes of luck as the sale of cows to Pees, and because of my continual trips out to the country which broke up the office routine, I might take a liking to the work. They thought it dangerous for a young man to have too much spare time; they distrusted my excessive reading and the resultant odd ideas.

As soon as I got to the office I spoke about the matter. The members of the firm and the accountant opined that Don Juan, in making the date with me, probably hadn't remembered that Thursday fell on the 25th, but they also said that if I didn't want to lose the sale I'd better appear on the appointed day. A man of his word, Don Juan was perfectly capable of renouncing a deal, no matter how lucrative it was, if the other party did not consummate the agreement down to the very last detail. One of the members of the firm commented:

"If because of negligence you lose the deal, it would be setting a bad precedent if we kept you in your position."

"If it's up to me, we won't lose it," I replied.

Since I had the Nash at my disposal, I wouldn't have given up the trip for anything. To start off in high style I had lunch at the hotel. The proprietress grouped all the diners at one end of a long table. Altogether we were about a half dozen: an older man, three or four traveling salesmen, and myself. They referred to the older man as "the passenger." From the very beginning I was leery of him. He looked exaggeratedly gentle, reminding me of certain images of saints. I considered him hypocritical and, so that he wouldn't be the center of attention, I began bantering about my business with Don Juan. I said:

"Tomorrow we're closing a deal."

"Tomorrow is Christmas," the passenger commented.

"So what's wrong with that?" I said.

"Don Juan's land is in Pardo," one of the traveling salesmen said, or asked.

"In Pardo."

"If you're going by car, through Cacharí, you should get going right away," said the salesman, and with a vague gesture he indicated the window.

Then I heard the rain, and saw it. It was raining cats and dogs.

"After a while nobody can pass through that road. I swear to you: not a soul."

I turned a deaf ear, because I don't like people to give me orders. I always had faith in my ability to drive in mud, but the wind was blowing from the east, and perhaps it would rain a lot. If I didn't want to get caught on the road at night, the best thing was to leave as soon as possible.

"I'm going," I said.

As I put on my rain slicker, the proprietress came over and said:

"A gentleman asked me to ask you if it wouldn't be a big bother to take him."

"Who?" I asked.

Predictably she answered:

"The gentleman passenger."

"Okay," I said.

"I'm glad. He's a strange man, but worldly, and on a trip like the one that awaits you, it's better not to be alone."

"Why?"

"A devilishly bad road. Anything can happen."

Before she could call for him, my travel companion appeared. He said with his unmistakable voice:

"My name is Swerberg. If you want I'll help you put the chains on."

"Who told him I was going to put them on?" I murmured with annoyance. Shaking my head, I looked in the tool box for the chains and the jack, and undertook the job at hand.

"I can handle it on my own," I answered.

Minutes later we set off on the trip. The road was heavy going, with marshes all around, and my companion's talkativeness irritated me. From time to time I felt obliged to answer him, but I wanted to direct all my attention to the route, from which I should not veer. A series of marshes, like the one we had ahead of us, is boring, even tiring, and the first careless move could lead one to commit errors. Of course the passenger spoke about Christmas and about the fact, for him nearly unthinkable, that Don Juan and I would meet on the 25th, to conclude a cattle deal.

"What are you suggesting?" I asked. "That my business with Don Juan is a mere lie, an invention to give myself importance, or to have a car loaned to me so that I can take a ride? A fine ride."

"I didn't think that you were lying. In any case I should make clear that it isn't so easy to distinguish between truth and lies. In time, many lies become truths."

"I don't like what you're saying," I replied.

"I'm terribly sorry," he answered.

"You're terribly sorry, but what you're telling me is that I'm lying. A lie is always a lie."

I think the passenger said under his breath: "There's where you're wrong." I ignored him and concentrated on the driving, on following the tracks, in third gear, at a slow speed. Not as slow as to risk having the engine stop at any resistance on the road. At a slow but steady speed, keeping the wheels on course, without ever veering from it. "I'm a virtuoso when it comes to driving in mud," I reflected. If I was irritated by this man, it wasn't because he distracted me from what I was doing, but because he was obliging me to listen to him and because he spoke in a tone that was both paternal and sleazy. He stated:

"In Europe, where I come from, nobody concludes deals on the 25th of December."

"I know. In the name of Don Juan, and in my own, may I beg forgiveness."

"I only mentioned the fact as proof of the difference in customs. In South America they don't know the spirit of Christmas. The day passes almost unnoticed, except for the children, who expect gifts. In Germany and in northern Europe, Santa Claus, whom some call Papa Noel, brings toys, all dressed in red, in a sled drawn by reindeer. For the child's imagination, is there any better gift than a legend like that?"

I rapidly searched for an answer that would in some way reveal my hostility. I finally said:

"As if they weren't told enough lies, now another is added. What are they trying to do? Have them not believe in anything?"

"Don't worry about it," he answered. "People don't abandon their beliefs so easily."

"Even though they know they're lies?"

On the other side of Los Huesos riverbed, the road was very bad and soon became an interminable swamp. The passenger said:

"You think we're going to get out of this swamp? It seems very tricky to me. Further on we're going to find even worse ones."

"You pick up one's spirits."

"The old swamps are tricky. How old the ones on this road must be to appear, name and all, on a map of the region."

"Have you seen the map?"

"The agent for the Guanaco mills saw it with his own eyes. A man like that does not talk just for the sake of talking."

We reached a stretch in which the ground, though muddy, was firmer. I said:

"Will we or won't we get out of this?"

"He had faith in himself and he succeeded. And you deny faith."

"If I'm not mistaken, what matters least is good driving."

I'm annoyed when my driving ability is not recognized.

The rain continued, and lightning flashed several times. The strongest flashes illuminated, for a few seconds, large caves opening among the clouds. The passenger affirmed:

"When there's lightning like this, people look at the

sky to see if in one of those holes they catch a glimpse of God or angels. There are those who say they saw them."

"And you believe them. Like the Guanaco agent."

"I turn the refrain around. Believing is seeing."

"Have you seen much?"

"More than you, my young friend, a little more. From all that I've lived. Also from my travels."

"The voice of authority."

"And also substance."

"What did you see in your trips that is worth talking about? Did you see God among the clouds?"

"If you ask me about the creator of heaven and earth, of course I'll answer that I didn't see him."

"A good thing."

"He retired after the Creation, so that we men could make of our earth what we want."

"I'll bet that you learned this from a good source. Is heaven empty now?"

"How could you think such a thing? Since the world has been the world, we have inhabited it with our gods. Tell me the truth: now do you begin to understand the importance of beliefs?"

I answered him, perhaps gruffly:

"For me, now, the only thing that's important is the swamp we're crossing."

It was thick, deep and, like some of the previous ones, it appeared to be endless.

"It's very bad," said the passenger. "If I were you, I'd switch into second."

"I didn't ask for advice."

"I know, but I suspect that we're going to get stuck. I won't discourage you. Keep going while you can."

"Of course I'm going to keep going."

Then came a long bumpy crossing in which the ups and downs were extremely important at the moment but soon forgotten.

"Are you angry?" he asked.

"You'd make anybody dizzy with your talk. Do you realize that?"

"I realize that you're a good driver. That's why, instead of worrying about the swamps, I'm going to talk to you about more elevated subjects. I'll begin by reminding you of the good news I just gave you. Heaven is not empty. It never was."

"How fortunate."

Don't ask me what happened. I must have gotten tired of driving carefully, or of the endless succession of swamps, or of the unanticipated information from the passenger. With a sure hand I drove in a carefree manner, which responded to passing impulses and allowed me to vent my feelings. The passenger did not stop talking. He was explaining:

"Heaven—now pay attention—is a projection of our imagination. Men place there the gods of their faith. There were periods in which the Egyptian gods reigned. They were evicted later on by the Greeks and Romans. Now our gods govern up there."

"Damn," I said and, upon seeing the surprised look on the passenger's face, I added: "There you have what happens by talking the ear off of the poor devil who's driving."

We were stuck. I tried to get out, going forward first, then going backward, but it was impossible. I realized that it would be better not to insist.

"Don't be impatient," he said.

I replied:

"You don't have to be in Pardo tomorrow."

"Maybe someone will show up and get us out."

"Have you seen other cars on the road? I haven't. Birds don't even pass by here."

"Then allow me to help out."

"Are you going to push?"

"We wouldn't get anywhere that way."

"I understand. It's raining, there's mud."

"I'm afraid you don't like my suggestions. You did what you could to get out and you were unable to, right? Let me try."

"Do you drive better?"

"It's not a matter of that."

"What's it a matter of?"

"Of letting another person try his luck. In any case, what can we do now? Wait and, according to you, futilely, because nobody passes through here. Of course, maybe you don't want to be in Pardo tomorrow.

"Not being in Pardo tomorrow would be for me a disaster."

"Then let me try."

Perhaps out of confusion I asked:

"To give you my place, I should open the door and throw myself into the swamp? It's clear that you don't want to get wet or muddy."

"It's not necessary," he said, and over the back of

his seat he slipped into the rear. "Move over, please."

He occupied my place, turned the starter, and before I could manage to formulate some advice we moved slowly, but resolutely, and very soon we reached an unexpected area of firm ground, where without a doubt it had rained very little. The passenger accelerated. I looked, with alarm, at the speedometer, and I heard the repeated knocking of a chain against the mudguard.

"Can't you hear?" I asked dryly. "Stop, man, stop. I'll take the chains off."

"I'll do it, if you want."

"No," I said.

I got out of the car. There was that light at dusk after a storm which infuses all the colors with intensity. I saw around me wide open country, brown where there was plowed farmland, the rest very green; the wire fences, blue and gray; a few cows, red and pink. When I released the chains I ordered:

"Move ahead."

He moved a meter or two. I picked up the chains, put them in the tool box and raised my eyes. The passenger was not in the car. As in that bare countryside there was no place to hide, I felt disoriented and in exasperation wondered if he had disappeared.

Cato

For years I said that Jorge Davel was a second-rate imitation of John Gilbert, another second-rate actor. As far as I was concerned, the many fans he had proved how arbitrary was fame, and how ironic was destiny that they called him "The Face." I used to remark, as if to prove the point, "By giving him that nickname, our audiences merely copy a vaster audience that calls some Hollywood hack 'The Profile.'"

I abandoned forever this sarcastic litany the night I saw him at The Smart Theater, co-starring with Paulina Singerman in *The Big Parade,* a stage adaptation of King Vidor's old film. During the play I also forgot about the review I was supposed to write for my paper, and even my own presence in the theater. Or rather I thought that, along with the heroes in *The Big Parade,* I was in the muddy trenches somewhere in France, listening to the bullets of the First World War whizz by.

Some time later I gave up journalism and got a job in the country, which I was felt to be suited for, because of my family background. I had no great hopes in the matter, but I thought that in solitude I might actually write the novel I had started several times in confidence and given up in despair.

On the ranch where I worked, La Cubana, during siesta I would read the newspaper. I often looked for any news of Davel, but in the three years I spent there I only found a few items. Davel had taken part in a benefit performance for an elderly actress; he had been seen at an actor's funeral and, if I remember correctly, at opening night of a comedy by García Velloso. I remember those bits, because I read them with the close attention we give to things we care about. I wonder if I wasn't trying to make amends, if only to myself, for the injustice I had done our great actor.

Back in Buenos Aires I published my novel. Whether because it had some success and because I was a well-known writer (while reviews were coming out and the book was in the bookstores), or because people still remembered that I had worked on the Entertainment Section of the paper, I was made member of a jury to award the best actors of the year. At the judges' meetings I struck up a friendship with Grinberg, author of the farce *His Latest Flame*. The evening we cast our votes, we were chatting in the café on the corner of Alsina and Bernardo de Irigoyen. I remember a remark Grinberg made:

"We awarded the best actors. But what a long way they all are from Davel! And just think, these days Davel isn't even working. Nobody offers him any parts."

I asked why, and he replied:

"They say he's old. That his only capital was his face. That all he had to do was to show it, and that he's no use now as a male lead."

"This country is hopeless."

"We've got a great actor, and nobody even realizes it."

"You and I do."

"And one or two others. Quartucci, for example, thinks that Davel is a theatrical miracle, one of those great actors who emerge once in a blue moon. He said to me: 'Whenever I have some time, I go to see him when he's at work, because he does it so naturally that he makes you think acting is the easiest thing in the world.'"

"So that makes three of us for Davel."

"You can count Caviglia in as well. One afternoon he'd been with Davel, chatting in the café, and later he saw him on the stage in *Summer Madness*. I think I can remember Caviglia's words: 'I caught myself thinking that Enrique was going to two-time his cousin.' See what I mean? He thought that the man before his eyes was Enrique, one of the characters in the comedy, not Davel. He insisted that nothing like that had ever happened to him, that he was a professional: If he went to the theater he concentrated on his job, and what's more he knew Laferrère's play by heart. Nevertheless, at that moment he was completely caught up in the dramatic illusion. He thought that only Davel could achieve this so powerfully."

After this chat other things came along that captured my attention for a long time. Despite those magic words

repeated by bookseller friends, "Your little novel is doing well," what it brought in was nowhere enough to live
on. I looked for a job, and when the savings I'd put away
in the country were about to run out, I found one. The
following years were hard, or at least thankless. When
I'd get home, after a day at the office, I was in no mood
for writing. But once in a while I'd pull myself together,
and at the end of a year of sporadic efforts repeated
week after week, I managed to produce a second novel,
shorter than the previous one. It was then that I became
acquainted with one of the bitter sides of our profession:
doing the rounds with a manuscript. Some editors didn't
seem to remember my first novel and listened with disbelief when I spoke of its success. Those who did remember
maintained that this one was not as good. To make it
clear that the interview was over they'd shake their
heads and say: 'You might as well chuck it. This second
book's a flop.'"

One day I met Grinberg in the café-bar La Academia. I
immediately thought of Davel and asked him for news.
He said:

"It's a sad story. First he sold his car, then the apartment. He's living in poverty. Another actor, who's in
a similar situation, told me they went on tour around
the provinces. They were practically living in station
waiting rooms, on coffee and buns. But this actor
assured me these hardships had had no effect on Davel's good humor. As long as he was working, he was
happy."

At the time of the dictatorship there were fewer and
fewer tours, until they finally ceased altogether. The en-

tire country came to a halt because people went into
retreat if they could, so as to be forgotten. Oblivion
seemed to be the best refuge in those days. Davel, too,
managed to be forgotten, though he himself wasn't looking for safety. He had no reason to, since he'd never been
involved in politics, not even the internal politics of the
Actors' Guild. Since helping him would neither support
a sympathizer nor ensure the gratitude of an opponent,
nobody gave him a hand. Davel spent most of that period without work.

Then came the day when I was pleasantly surprised to
read, I forget where, that Davel was to have the title role
in *Cato*, a famous tragedy whose revival was announced
at the Politeama theater, for the forthcoming season.
One evening that same week I discussed the news with
Grinberg.

"Things happen when you least expect them to," he
declared.

"I was coming to that," I said. "It seems strange that
nowadays an impresario should remember this gem of
classical repertoire, and really incredible that he should
hit on Davel to play the part of Cato."

"Not all the credit should go to him."

He went on to explain that the impresario, a certain
Romano, had chosen the tragedy of *Cato* because the
author, who'd been dead for two hundred years, could
not claim copyright.

"That still leaves him the credit of choosing Davel," I
remarked.

"His wife, who had once been Davel's girlfriend, recommended him."

I must have looked annoyed, because Grinberg asked me what was the matter.

"Nothing . . . I feel admiration, almost affection for Davel, and I'd like the story of this stroke of luck to be entirely aboveboard."

Even though Grinberg was short, twitched constantly, and in general looked slovenly and feeble, you had to respect the power of his intellect.

"What you might like is of little importance," he assured me. "It's undoubtedly noble and generous for a woman to ask her husband to do an ex-lover a favor when he's down on his luck."

"I admit that she . . ."

"Admit the same for them all. Davel, because he asks for nothing and because an ex-lover feels inspired to come to his defense when passion is gone. The impresario, because he behaves like a true professional. A good actor's suggested to him, and he takes him on without bothering about personal matters."

On the first night, the Politeama was nearly sold out. I remember clearly that when the play began I had a few minutes' suspense, in which I said to myself: "This could still be either a triumph or a flop. I'll soon know which." And in fact I didn't have to wait long. I won't say I thought the play was bad. Without denying that it's rich in lofty epic moments, I felt it was less a tragedy than a dramatic poem, very literary no doubt, and quite boring. The hero's situation certainly provoked anxiety, but the plot loses momentum when the author unexpectedly inserts a love story, which is as unbelievable as it is stupid. It's curious that as I was thinking: "Now that Davel's been lucky enough to get work, he should have been

luckier with the play," I was looking at Cato, I mean
Davel in the role of Cato, and I'd have given anything for
him to defeat Caesar and to save Utica. Yes, I was even
anxious about the fate of the city of Utica, and at that
moment I actually wanted the power, not even granted
to the gods, to change the past. In Davel's face (which I'd
once called trivial), one of those faces that improve with
age, I clearly saw the nobility of the hero ready to die for
republican liberty. When one of Cato's sons—a very un-
convincing actor—said: "Our father is fighting for
honor, for virtue, for liberty, and for Rome," I could
barely hold back my tears.

At this point the reader probably feels that any cri-
tique of mine is superfluous. The play's success, and its
increasing impact on its audiences, certainly support
such an opinion. From the third or fourth night on, the
theater was packed. You had to reserve seats fifteen or
twenty days in advance, which was highly unusual in the
Buenos Aires of those days. Another unusual thing was
that the spectators unanimously interpreted the invectives against Caesar as invectives against our dictator
and the call for the liberty of Rome as the call for our lost
freedom. I am sure they read that meaning into it simply
because they wanted to. If, as someone once said, all
readers read the books they want to read, these performances at the Politeama prove that we can say the same
of audiences and plays. Do not imagine that when speaking of audiences I exclude myself . . . Again I felt tears
in my eyes when Cato said: "There is no Rome now. Oh
liberty! Oh virtue! Oh my country!"

Each night the play's success grew noisier and wilder.
At one point I wondered whether the disturbances at the

Politeama, though inspired in the best of intentions, might not—why deny it?—be harmful to our cause. The government could easily close the theater, and, by the same token, gain a political advantage. Indeed, the moderates might silently approve of such a move through an atavistic fear of excess, even though they were as against the dictatorship as we were.

For many the identification of Davel with Cato was complete. In the street people would say to him: "Hello Cato," and sometimes, "Long live Cato!"

Those of us who in one way or another are involved in the theater probably exaggerate the influence those performances at the Politeama had on succeeding events, but the conspirators certainly believed in that influence too. I know, because they gave me the task of talking to Davel to get his support for our cause. We wanted to say, in the hour of triumph, that our great actor had always been on the side of the revolution. We wanted to say it without lying and without laying ourselves open to the possibility of his denying it.

I arranged to meet him in the café on the corner of Alsina and Bernardo de Irigoyen. Yes, the old song was right, I thought, the changes brought by the years are indeed strange: Davel's face now hardly recalled John Gilbert's but rather was much more like Charles Laughton's. His expression was sad and tired, but also revealed patient and boundless determination. In any case, when I told him that my admiration for him had begun on the first night of *The Big Parade,* at the Smart, I could swear he looked younger and a bit like John Gilbert again. He asked insistently:

"Did you really think I was up to the part?"

"Beforehand, I thought the play could never compete with the film. But even without the help of the location shots in the film, the audience at the Smart really believed you were at the battlefront. I'd go further: you yourself took us to the front."

After a while I ventured to ask him if he gave us his support.

"Of course," he replied. "I'm against tyranny. Don't you remember what I say in the second act?"

"In the second act of *Cato?*"

"Where else? Listen carefully. I say: 'Until there come better times, the sword must remain unsheathed and sharpened, to receive Caesar.'"

At first I liked the reply. I took the bravado of it as a pledge of faith and courage. Afterward, for some reason I don't understand, I wasn't so sure. "But at least the reply is affirmative," I said to myself. "That's something."

The government must have taken the uproarious performances at the Politeama seriously, because one evening the police arrested the manager, the director, and the actors, and closed down the theater. Next morning they let them all go, except the manager and Davel. Finally they released the manager. And the actor, a few days later. I suspect that they did not forgive him for his role as enemy of the dictatorship and that they released him because they themselves realized he was only an actor.

Contrary to what I'd anticipated, the closing of the Politeama was damaging to the government. Perhaps people thought that if the government attached so much importance to a play, it must be very frightened and very weak.

We interpreted this conjecture as the truth and, from then on, began conspiring out in the open. First in private houses, then in restaurants, there were a lot of very crowded banquets, always attended by the ringleaders of the movement and at which the speakers demanded and promised revolution. At these long tables Davel always had a prominent place; not at the head of the table, of course, but always seated on the right of some celebrity.

One day a woman telephoned me, and said:

"You don't know me. I'm Romano's wife, Luz Romano. I've got to speak to you in person."

For lack of imagination, or by force of habit, I arranged to meet her in the café on the corner of Alsina and Bernardo de Irigoyen.

She was a very attractive woman, not particularly young, tall, calm, dark-haired, with a pale complexion and beautiful eyes that looked you straight in the face. She said to me:

"You're using Davel. When politicians do this, I'm not surprised. One expects them to be unscrupulous. But you're a writer."

"What's that got to do with it?"

"You're not only using him: you're putting him at risk."

"Davel put himself at risk from the very first night of *Cato*," I replied without lying.

"I agree. And it was my fault."

"I didn't say that."

"You didn't say it, but it's true. Nevertheless, there's a difference. I only asked that he should be offered a part. You sought him out to use him for political purposes. A destiny Davel did not choose."

"But which he does not find inappropriate. He's identified with his role. He wants to fight the dictatorship."

"Such a conviction, in his case, cannot be compared with yours, nor with that of a politician, nor was it formed in the same way. Davel is still acting."

In self-defense, I said:

"We're all acting."

"Yes, but now you're equivocating. Do you know what you're doing?"

"We're inviting a citizen to take part in our struggle."

"You mean you're asking an innocent man to get himself killed."

"You're exaggerating, and you're being very hard on me."

"You're hard on Davel."

Until Luz spoke to me, these truths, which I had always known, had not bothered me. But now, the realization that I had acted wrongly filled me with anxiety. Luckily there was no cause for further remorse, since the revolution triumphed without anything happening to Davel.

We didn't forget him. At all the celebrations he had a place of honor. I offered him, at the suggestion of the new authorities, posts in Cultural Administration and other government departments. He didn't accept them. He said he only wanted to work in the theater. The directors of the state theater assured me they fully intended to satisfy that wish.

One evening I met Davel at a Press Club dinner. Like two veterans of the same campaign, we recalled incidents from the period of the dictatorship. At a certain moment I said:

"It seems unbelievable that all those things took place. And it also seems unbelievable that it's over. It was a nightmare." After a pause, I added: "The country's in your debt for what you did."

"We all did our part."

"Probably, but there was no nerve center of agitation like the Politeama theater. I know only too well how much we owe you."

"What more can an actor ask for than the audience's acclaim? They nearly brought the house down. I shall never forget it."

The conversation continued along parallel grooves: Davel talked to me about his work as an actor and I, about his work for the cause. Finally he admitted:

"When everyone says what terrible times those were, I feel tempted to comment: 'Not for me.' Just think: I had a part which gave me all sorts of satisfaction, in a play I liked and which was a huge success. Don't tell anyone this, but for me those dreadful times were wonderful."

"Of course," I said deliberately, so that my words would get through to his conscience, "what more can one ask for, but to be successful in one's work, and for a noble cause?"

"Yes," he agreed, "I was successful in my work, which is the main thing."

I was about to give up the exchange, when in a sudden outburst of irritation, I asked myself: "Why don't I force this thick-head to get my point?"

"I agree that it's good to entertain an audience," I said, "but . . . you don't mean to say there's nothing more important than the theater, do you?"

"If I didn't believe this I wouldn't be a good actor."

"So you think this because it's in your interest to think it?"

"No, I really believe it."

"That's very arrogant."

"The world can't function the way it should unless each of us believes in the importance of what we do."

"On that point we're in agreement."

"I don't want you to be deceived. For me the theater's the most important thing there is. Do you remember what Hamlet says? I do, because I've played Hamlet." He was silent for a moment and when he started speaking again, without raising his voice, he said: "Good my lord, will you see the players well bestowed? Do you hear, let them be well used, for they are the abstract and brief chronicles of the time."

His histrionic talent was so extraordinary that at that moment it seemed to me that Davel was speaking from a stage and that I was in the audience.

I'd never been to so many dinners as I went to then. At one of them, a fundraising event for the Actors' Benevolent Society, I found myself sitting between fatso Barilari, the party treasurer, "an unrepentant campaigner," on his own admission, and a thin and excitable young man, who turned out to be Walter Pérez. During the underground years, his name had often come up, usually preceded or followed by the word *activist*. I also link the expression *dynamite* with it, I don't know why. Barilari described Walter as "the most intolerant of the supporters of liberty." I have to admit that he kept me and my fat neighbor amused throughout the whole meal, with stories of the clashes between his group and guys from other parties. Those stories do not seem so funny to me now.

At the opposite end of the table, Luz Romano and Davel were talking. I would have gladly sat down next to them. That evening Luz looked particularly attractive. As we were leaving the table, she came up to me and murmured:

"Congratulations on your young friend."

"Who do you mean?"

"Who else but Walter, of course."

"A useful individual," I said, repeating my fellow comrades' expression, "he cares about the cause for freedom."

"Cares about it too much. He believes in ideas, and isn't concerned about people."

"A philosopher, then."

"A fanatic."

"The party is fighting for sensible ideas. More to the point would be to express our envy and bitterness."

"So you admit that Walter's out of place with your lot?"

"I'm only trying to say that every party needs a drop

of dogmatism and even of extremism from time to time. There are plenty of occasions when fellows like Pérez are useful."

When Romano came over, Luz took him by the arm and stormed off. Her manner left me somewhat confused.

As for Davel, he again went several years without work, in poverty. As I've already said, at the national theaters they listened to my recommendations with plenty of good will, but for one reason or another they did not engage him. And the managers of the other theaters did not remember him either. Fortunately we did show him tokens of gratitude. He was our guest of honor at an endless succession of official ceremonies, and at quite a few banquets. Of course when we saw him dressed in the same very old and barely respectable suit, we couldn't help feeling a mixture of irritation and guilt.

Since history always repeats itself, one day I heard the good news that Romano had engaged Davel, to put *Cato* on again. On this occasion, the theater was to be the Apollo.

Shortly afterward, early one evening as I was leaving the office, someone called. Despite the fact that the sound was muffled by the connection, I recognized Luz Romano's voice. What I understood was that we had to meet so that she could ask me for something. We were cut off. I had divided feelings: I wanted to see her and was curious about her, but I was afraid to be bothered with tiresome requests. She rang again, on several occasions. My secretary always said I was away or at a meeting. Those short but numerous conversations led to a sort of friendship, and in the end Luz explained to her why she was calling.

When my secretary gave me the message, I muttered: "Women! The ideas they get into their heads!" Luz Romano was actually asking our government to prohibit—no more, no less—the revival of *Cato*.

I presumed that the absent-minded Davel must have ingenuously hurt her feelings, and turned the affection Luz had always had for him into hatred.

The events that followed the revival of *Cato* proved the woman's request had not been unjustified. Night after night the audiences grew more enthusiastic and more threatening. I must admit that at the beginning it was hard for us to grasp the fact that they were applauding against us. It seemed impossible they were using that tragedy to attack a government whose chief merit was the restoration of liberties.

At a party at the house of mutual friends, Luz gave me the explanation. The people who were applauding at the Apollo were officials and supporters of the dictatorship. It was their own lost freedom that they were demanding back.

"They must have a Walter Pérez too," she said.

"What do you mean, a Walter Pérez?" I asked.

"Don't pretend you don't understand."

"I don't understand."

"It's quite clear. If you sent Walter along as the agitators' emcee at the first *Cato* . . ."

"What happened at the Politeama was spontaneous," I protested.

"With Walter leading it. You can be sure the present lot have got a fanatic like him to rely on."

"It's not fair to mention that young champion of freedom in the same breath as a hired rabble-rouser of the dictatorship."

"Spoken like a true politician, but you'll have to agree with me on this: What can a noble cause mean to a thug like Walter Pérez?"

I didn't tell her that she was talking like a schoolmarm, but I said, taking in the others as well:

"I just feel sad that an actor we did so much for should now allow himself to be used against us."

"A betrayal," exclaimed someone.

"I wouldn't go as far as that," I amended. "I'll only say that I regard his behavior with a certain bitterness."

About a week later, in the middle of the night, I was awakened by the phone. A woman's voice said:

"Happy now?"

What I was, was sleepy, so that I found it difficult to understand. I repeated the question like an idiot:

"Who is it?" (A pointless question, because I had guessed who was calling.)

"Tell me if you're happy," she insisted, and then, after a pause, "Or haven't you heard?"

"I don't know what you're talking about."

Luz said:

"Then you'd better wait."

"Wait for what?"

"You'll find out tomorrow."

She hung up. I was about to call her, but I held back. I guessed what had happened, although I kept muttering: "It's not possible."

Next day I knew it all. It's odd: I was prepared for the news, yet I felt disoriented. As disoriented as the night before, when I guessed it, and very sad. As though an old friend had died. In anticipation, perhaps, of an article or a speech, I told myself that this death marked the end of the most brilliant period of Argentine theater.

The newspaper accounts were fairly comprehensive, and my friends in the Ministry of the Interior told me the rest. The incident occurred toward the end of the last act of the evening performance. After plunging the sword into his own body, the dying Cato is worried about the fate of those who took part with him in the resistance against Caesar. He listens to their plans of escape and gives them his blessing, bids them farewell and dies. At that moment a shot rang out. There was a great commotion in the house. Some people pointed to a box. Someone hastily got up and left another box. At first no one knew what had happened. Then, everyone learned that Davel had died of a bullet wound, probably fired from a balcony box. The police found Walter Pérez there, with two of his men. None of them was armed. As for the one who'd left from the other box, he managed to disappear.

I was asked to speak at the Chacarita Cemetery. I refused because I was upset and because I felt it should be done by someone who knew more about the theater and was close to the hearts of the actors. Romano, in his speech, said that the best end for an actor is to die on stage, at the moment of his character's death. A representative of the government spoke as well. Grinberg, who appeared out of nowhere and startled me when he took me by the arm, remarked in a murmur:

"It's a bit late now to show respect."

The Navigator
Returns to His Country

I think I saw *A Passage to India* because my country was in the title of the movie. Upon leaving the theater, I took the subway—or Metro, as they call it here—to go to the Embassy, where every day I work a few hours. What I earn there allows me certain extravagances that brighten up my life as a poor student. I suspect that because of those extravagances, I sometimes fall into a kind of somnambulism which usually provokes disturbing situations. Here's an example: upon remembering the subway trip, I see myself comfortably sitting, even though I have proof that I was standing, near the doors, grasping the iron pole and on the verge of falling whenever the train stops or starts up. From there I look, with a mixture of contempt and commiseration, upon a Cambodian student dressed in tattered rags, in a seat in the middle of the car, dozing as he leans his head against the window. His hair, as abundant as it is dirty, reveals a bald and wrinkled circle, and his three- or four-day beard is sparse. He smiles in his sleep, moves his lips quickly and gently, as if in a whisper he were maintaining a friendly conversation with himself. I think: "He seems happy, although there is no reason for him to be so. He lives, like me, among hostile Europeans. As much as they might try to hide it, they are hostile to those they judge to be different. In this sense we Indians have some advantage, for being less different, but who doesn't have an advantage over this boy, who looks so singular? Even if he were a Westerner and from the north, he would be considered a representative of the scum of the earth. Not even I, who consider myself free of prejudices, would venture to trust him."

I get off at La Muette station and immediately find myself on Rue Alfred-Dehodencq, where the Embassy is located. As incredible as it seems, the doorman doesn't recognize me and refuses to let me pass. As we scuffle with bare fists, the man shouts: "Out of here! Out!" several times. One of the last times, the shout turns into a friendly "Sour-sday" which in Cambodian means, "Good morning." I open my eyes and still perplexed I see my friend the taxi driver, a countryman, who is shaking me to wake me up, and who repeats the greeting and adds: "We have to get out. We're coming to our stop." I stand up and almost trip as I leave the car; I follow my countryman along the platform, without asking anything, for fear of making a mistake and having him believe I'm crazy or drugged. Before going up the stairs, when we pass in front of the mirror, I have a revelation, no less painful though foreseen. I mean that the mirror reflects my dirty hair, my sparse three- or four-day beard; but what frankly bothers me is realizing that also at this moment I am moving my lips and, what's even worse, I am smiling as I talk to myself, like an idiot.

Our Trip (A Diary)

Selection, Prologue, and Epilogue by F. B.

PROLOGUE

The editor of Jackson House had told me that he was preparing a collection of travel diaries and that if I had one I should send it on to him. When I reread mine from 1960 and 1964, for reasons I don't know how to explain, I somehow didn't feel like publishing them. I then proposed *Our Trip* by Lucio Herrera. To tell the truth I was afraid it would be rejected since it did not correspond to the expectations of those who read works of this genre. But they accepted and included it in one of the beautiful volumes—bound in red imitation leather with gold letters—of one of the many collections that Jackson House sold, along with its polished wood bookcase. As the travel diary of my friend Herrera probably sleeps in the waiting room of people who don't read, beside Timon's *Book of Orators*, the tomes of Willie Durant, the illustrated hundredth anniversary edition of *Don Quixote* and a *Martin Fierro* bound in golden cowhide, I decided to publish it in this volume, on sale in good bookstores.

F. B.

OUR TRIP (Lucio Herrera's Diary)

Buenos Aires. Puerto Nuevo. January 3 1968.
I am pleasantly surprised to find amidst the crowd the round, brick-colored face and round dark eyes of Paco Barbieri. "You're also traveling in the *Pasteur?*" I ask him. How nice to have him as a travel companion. I introduce him to Carmen. A bit later, when we go up the gangway ladder, Carmen asks: "Is he traveling alone?" "I think so." "Could your friend be a little strange?" "No, not in the sense you're thinking of." "In what sense then?" "Why should we go into this? Each one is the way he is." "How stupid I am. I never thought you had secrets from me. I thought you loved me just as I love you." So as not to begin the trip with a fight, I sacrifice the friend. "Look," I answer, "I don't know how to explain it to you. Barbieri is not a conventional guy. He says that women are the tax we pay for pleasure." "And because he speaks such nonsense, you think he's not conventional? I would say he's a typical macho pig, which in this country is nothing out of the ordinary. So as not to travel with a woman, the idiot travels alone?" "Yes, even though he'd never admit it." "A liar besides? A macho pig and a liar. Let me tell you that I'm beginning to get tired of your friend." "He travels with an inflatable doll." "I don't believe you! If that's true, he's

very sick. He needs talking to right away. If you won't talk to him, I will." "I'm asking you not to do it. Please, let's not interfere." "Okay. It's your friend. A fine friend. Thinking it over carefully, maybe you're right. It's best not to touch a degenerate like that, not even with a ten-foot pole." I assure her that Paco is a good person. She mocks me, as she answers angrily: "Aside from all that he's a good person? Don't talk nonsense. Since we shouldn't interfere, do me the favor of keeping him at a distance during the whole trip." "Do you know what you're asking of me? Paco is my best friend." "Stay with your best friend. I'll die of sadness, but what does that matter? My only consolation is that you're not going to have your Paco for long. A sick man with such neuroses breaks down sooner or later."

On board the PASTEUR, *on the open sea. January 14.*
Not only Paco Barbieri awakens her animosity. Carmen, taking her time but with relentless consistency, proceeds to tear to pieces with all sorts of mockery and slanderous accusations any friend I mention. I try not to speak, in front of her, about people for whom I feel affection.

Rome. February 8.
We had agreed to eat early, to be on time for the concert, which begins at nine. Celia tells me that it bothers her when I watch her dress and brush her hair. I go down to the hotel reception room. I leaf through magazines, get bored and after a while, tired of waiting, I call the elevator, to go get her. When the door opens Celia appears, so dazzlingly beautiful that I forget the reproaches I had

planned as I waited, I take her in my arms, give her a kiss and say to her: "Thank you for being so pretty." We walk to the Archimedes restaurant, to eat there, like every night, but before reaching the little Caprettari Square we stop to read the menu of a French restaurant. As I see that today's dessert is *baba au chocolat,* I ask Celia: "What do you think about going here?" "I can't believe it," she exclaims. "I thought you would never take me to another restaurant, that for you the only one was the Archimedes." As you can already tell, Celia reproaches my supposed whim to return always to the same restaurant; but it's not out of mere whim that I take her, twice daily, to the Archimedes. If in one place they feed us well and treat us like regular customers, wouldn't it be absurd to try others and end up poisoned? Celia looks suspiciously upon the restaurants I prefer. As if I weren't aware of the implicit condemnation in her response, I explain: "The thing is that here they have *baba au chocolat* for dessert, and you know how much I like it." We entered, we ordered our food, which luckily deserved Celia's approval. The second course finished, the waiter asks us what we would like for dessert. I answer: "Two *babas au chocolat.*" "I'm very sorry. There's no time," Celia declares and orders the waiter to bring the bill. I don't know what has gotten into her: her most deep-rooted habit is always to arrive late, no matter where she goes, but today she wants us to leave for the concert a half-hour early. Since the theater is not far away, we get there immediately. "We had time to eat our *baba au chocolat,*" I observe. She agrees with me but adds: "Let's not cry over that." Of course not, but neither am I going to hide something that bothers me and, why deny it, that I resent. I think: "There's good reason why kids don't like to go without their dessert." Pavarotti's recital is long. The audience applauds with all its might. I must admit that I don't understand much about music, but toward the end there's a song I like a lot, and it even makes me feel like keeping time with the rhythm by moving my head, my hands, and even my whole body. I discover that it's called *Sole mio* or something like that.

Rome, February 9.
Today we're off to the movies. They're playing an old film, *The Man Who Could Work Miracles.* I am very amused by it. Celia is not amused. I suspect that not only the movie annoys her; as incredible as it seems, I suspect that I too annoy her with my unrestrained laughter. I must admit that upon noting her insensitivity to the merits of this film I feel sad, and even offended. I get to the point of thinking that as we sit there next to each other we are separated by an abyss. There's an irresistibly comic scene in which the main character, in the salon of a London club, makes a lion appear before his fellow members, who pass from skepticism over his miracles to a true state of alarm. What is Celia's commentary about this situation? "I can't stand it any longer. This scene is not in Wells's story." I can't believe she is making such a pedantic comment. She continues: "What lack of respect for the author! What a lack of integrity!" One can hear vehement hisses from the audience. "This movie is totally stupid," Celia asserts, without being intimidated. "Let's go." Very unpleasantly surprised, even amazed at

my bad luck, I follow her out of the theater. An hour later, as we're getting undressed in our hotel room, she turns toward me and as if a very strange idea suddenly occurred to her, she asks: "Did it bother you to leave before the movie was over?" "Quite a lot," I say to her. As if talking to herself, she reflects: "Not eating the *baba au chocolat* annoyed you. Not seeing the end of that stupid movie annoyed you. All men are little boys."

Verona. February 11.
As she casually leafs through the *Blue Guide,* Pilar comments: "We should see the tomb of the Scaligero." Suddenly her face lights up and she exclaims: "How could I forget them?" "Who?" I ask. "Who else? The lovers!" Immediately she makes me follow her to Juliet's tomb, which is not far, but not near either. She says I should stand on one side, and her on the other; we clasp our hands over the tomb and swear to love each other eternally. "And truly," says Pilar. "And truly," I repeat, to which I add: "Of course I'm not sure that the best place to swear true love is over a false tomb." "Where do you get the idea that it's false?" "From your guidebook. When you read it a little more carefully you'll see that it says: *the supposed tomb of Juliet.* As for the famous love of the woman who is not buried here, and of her Romeo, just think what it might have been: any old love, exaggerated by writers, and made into something sublime by people's enthusiasm for prodigies." Had I known how my observations would affect her, I would have kept quiet. She declares that there's nothing I like better than to destroy illusions ("The best thing that one

can have"), that I am "disagreeably negative," and that perhaps what I'm trying to tell her is that I don't love her.

Paris. February 15.
A warm night, for this time of year. On Rue Galilée we are returning from the movies, back to the hotel. Mentally I'm saying to myself: "Take it easy. Don't get impatient. You'll soon be getting what you like the most. I am so absent-minded, or the street is so quiet and empty, that Justina's voice takes me by surprise. "A penny for your thoughts?" she asks. "I don't know . . ." "How can you not know? It must have been something very beautiful, because you were smiling." "I was thinking," I say as I look at her expectant, trusting face which is so beautiful that for a few seconds I forget what I'm going to say . . . I recover my composure and continue: "I was thinking that luckily we'll soon be doing what we like best and that an incomparable sense of well-being will come afterward, a true bliss that will make us slip imperceptibly into sleep." I feel inspired, poetically inspired, upon pronouncing my little speech. Together, at night, in Paris, so far from the world of our routines: isn't it like getting married again and reaching another high point in our lives? Her voice takes me by surprise, this second time, in a different way. "I thought you went to bed with me because you loved me," she says. "But no: it's to feel good, to sleep better. For that men always went out looking for prostitutes." "How nice it would be to discover that she's only joking," I think. But she's serious. "The most convenient thing would be to marry

a prostitute. Still more convenient if she doesn't get offended. I'm offended." My only hope is that she'll get over her anger. But she doesn't. In silence we reach the hotel, go up to the room, get into bed. I hear her breathing. I look at her: she has fallen asleep, with a brow that expresses fury. I have to look for a way out of the situation. I attempt the recourse that never fails. Very gently I turn her on her back, separate her legs, embrace her. She pushes me away, perhaps without anger, but with sadness. She says to me: "You didn't understand me. You have offended me. Frivolous people forget insults. I don't." She turns her back on me and peacefully goes back to sleep.

Paris. February 16.
While I'm waiting for Justina, I chat, at the hotel reception desk, with the Rumanian girl who works there. She tells me that a very proper and pleasant Argentinian had been in the hotel just recently, a Señor Paco Barbieri. When Justina comes down, the Rumanian is telling me that Paco had been quite ill, with the flu. Upon hearing this Justina comments: "I told you so. He'll soon have a breakdown."

Paris. February 17.
In a *Sport-Dimanche* that somebody left in the waiting room of the Hotel de Roma I was able to find out that today Reims plays Paris-Saint-Germain a match that I wouldn't want to miss for anything, because Reims number 9—the center forward, as we'd say in my day—is none other than Carlitos Bianchi. After reading that, I

keep reminding her of my firm proposal to go on Sunday the 17th to the Parc aux Princes stadium: a tactic meant to soften things up, so that Justina understands that I'm not going to be available to go to the Louvre or to a concert at the Pleyel recital hall. Concerning my intentions, my tactic had good results. Justina knows that I'm going to the soccer game. What I didn't foresee is that by giving her time to think about the matter, she might come up with the unexpected idea of accompanying me to the game. She thought of it of course and of course I accepted complacently. No matter where we are, I always feel happy beside her. The fact that she's so pretty helps. I won't deny that at least mentally, I'm showing her off . . . Nor should I hide that in general I'm against going to sports events with women. Today I find out that I'm right about that. At the beginning Justina pretends to be interested and asks for explanations that disturb my concentration on the game. "What is a penalty?" "What is a corner?" "Why did they stop?" Afterward, in the midst of an extraordinary play by Carlitos, who dodges the defenses by Paris-Saint-Germain and scores a goal for history, I answer: "Of course, of course, but you'll agree with me that there's no goalie like Bianchi." I must be a big dreamer because I imagine that I can talk about soccer with the woman I love. She responds with a question: "Bianchi? Who is that? Another friend of yours?" In the second period she's so bored that she gets impatient, and before the game's over, with the excuse that we should avoid the crowds, she takes me by a hand, gets up, says to me: "Let's go, let's go." I have no choice but to follow her. It makes me indignant

to think that she'll never know the sacrifice she's impos-
ing on me. In my heart of hearts I'm a martyr, because
I'm leaving the stadium at this moment, and an ascetic,
because I don't utter even one word of complaint.

Paris. February 20.
Justina fell into bed with a bad cold, which soon turned
into the flu. "I caught it at that game which seemed like it
was never going to end," she complains. I go to the
movies, I have a pleasant time; nevertheless I miss her. I
reconsider the matter: "I shouldn't miss her. A woman
like her, first she ruins your spirit, then your health. The
only solution is divorce." I know it, but I can't resolve to
do so . . . At moments, to give myself courage, I appeal to rather absurd reflections. "It's a matter of life or
death," I say, as if I believed it. I walk alone on the
streets of Paris, in a state of calm, though like a wander-
ing soul in hell.

Manresa. Montserrat. February 24.
We pass by Manresa, a city surrounded by vineyards.
Luisita asks me, "Stop in front of that café." "We're
going to be late." "It doesn't matter. I want to have a
carajillo. To give me strength, you know. Who says that
Montserrat won't be uphill!" "It'll be just fine." We
entered the café. To be on the safe side I don't say a
thing; Luisita orders: "Two *carajillos*, please." The man
asks: "With rum or cognac?" We're in the midst of that
when, unbelievably (did the *carajillo* make me drunk?),
I see Paco Barbieri, walking toward the counter. I get up,
we hug. He looks tired, as if aged, his face less ruddy

than usual. He accompanies me to the table. Perhaps because he's tired or because Luisita makes no effort to detain him, he leaves immediately. Thinking out loud I murmur: "I'm sorry he's leaving so soon." "I'm not," Luisita answers: "Did you see how he is?" "I'll admit he seemed a little tired." "A little tired? He's a wreck. The living dead." "God forbid," I say to her. She replies: "I'll bet you anything that you won't see him again. Alive, I mean." On the road to Montserrat I don't open my mouth. If I have to answer something, I limit myself to monosyllables. Luisita doesn't ask me what's the matter. Upon reaching Montserrat, she says: "Let's leave the car here." "Shall we go up on foot?" "Fine." We're going up the hill, but very soon she admits that she can't climb any further. "Me neither," I say. For once, Luisita and I are in agreement. We stop a bus. It takes us up to the top; a while later we come down. We're so tired that, upon passing the place we left the car, we almost forget to ask the driver to stop. In Manresa, Luisita tells me: "I want another *carajillo.*" When we enter the café a second encounter with a friend occurs: Mileo, a fifth-year companion from the Mariano Moreno secondary school, who before reaching legal age had set up a factory to make headlights, which provoked my admiration. I ask him: "Are you still copying the Marshall headlights?" "You remember?" he says to me. "It was a dream of youth that didn't last long. From one day to the next the mudguards, the running boards, the exposed headlights, and I found myself making accessories for nonexistent automobiles." I tell him: "Guess who we were with a while ago? With Paco Barbieri." "I was too.

And you know the brilliant idea he had? Going up to Monserrat on foot. He was a wreck." "There's an acquaintance of mine here who had the same idea," I say, pointing to Luisita. "Luckily it didn't take long for her to throw in the towel, and we went up the rest of the way in a bus." As soon as Mileo leaves, Luisita observes: "I don't know which I'd choose. The degenerate or the dreamer of unusable automobile accessories. A nice sampling of friends." I think that on the whole way back to Barcelona we didn't speak again.

Rio de Janeiro. March 15.
It appears that the boat is going to pick up a lot of cargo and that we won't embark till tomorrow morning. I suggest an excursion to Petropolis. Margarita wants to go to the Copacabana beach. I let her have her way: a swim in the ocean is pleasant and less tiring than a car trip. We have lunch at a hotel. Then I accompany Margarita in her shopping. I don't know how she manages to take a whole afternoon to buy only three or four things. To take *our* whole afternoon, I should say. Waiting for her in several stores tired me out completely. What I want to do most is to get into bed. To my misfortune the waitress had given Margarita an address where tonight we can see a very interesting *macumba*. "The real thing. Not those *macumbas* for tourists, which everybody has seen." I argue the best I can, but in vain: I tell her that all *macumbas* are a fraud. Margarita gets angry, calls me a coward, and is upset by my lack of curiosity. I face tonight's program—why deny it?—with the most absolute lack of curiosity and with a reluctance close to fear.

After dining on the boat, we take a taxi in the direction of a neighborhood called the Old City: very poor, very populated. The houses—the operative word here is huts—are made of wood. We stop in front of one that has a top floor. We go up the steep staircase and enter a narrow corridor toward one door. Margarita opens it, saying "May I," and we enter a round little living room. I think I can safely say that the people there all look at us with disapproval. In the center some women are dancing, or rather whirling around, and they finally fall in the midst of epileptic convulsions. Girls in wide skirts with pleated ruffles pick them up. There's a man, a kind of leader, a mulatto, who turns out to be the priest. I don't know why, perhaps out of nervousness, Margarita starts laughing. Furious women mill around, and a man insinuates the gesture of taking out a weapon. If the *macumbero* didn't take us under his protection, anything could have happened to us. The man says to us: "Now it's better for you to go away. If they offer you something to smoke or drink, don't accept it. Don't enter any café. Don't take the first taxi you see, but the one I'm going to call for you." As we go down the creaking staircase, Margarita whispers to me: "Don't trust that sorcerer. Let's not wait for the taxi he called. He might want to kidnap us." Before I can prevent it, Margarita runs across the street and gets into a taxi. The taxi driver closes the door and, the tires squealing, he sweeps Margarita away at top speed, to rob her, to kidnap her, to rape or kill her, who knows? I look all around me in desperation and I see that a taxi is arriving, probably the *candombero*'s. I get in, as well as I can I explain, and we take off at such a crazy pace that I wonder if the driver is trying to frighten me so that I don't notice that the chase is useless. No sooner do I formulate such thoughts when I see that we are catching up with the other car, whose driver opens a door and with one push throws out Margarita. We nearly run over her. We pick her up trembling and sobbing, her face swollen. With great difficulty I persuade the taxi driver to renounce the chase. "The lady is very frightened," I explain. She must be because upon hearing this she doesn't protest.

On board the PASTEUR. *March 17. In the afternoon.*
Lately Emilia's character has gotten worse. At her side I suffer a regime of setbacks and vexations capable of destroying anybody's health. I have to leave her. She will get sad when I announce this, of that I'm sure; I'm also sure that upon seeing her sadness, my determination will falter. To not turn back, from the boat I send a telegram to a lawyer, Doctor Sivori, and ask him to negotiate my separation.

March 19, at night. On board the PASTEUR. *Gulf of Santa Catalina.*
Rough sea. In pajamas, barefoot, we're packing our suitcases. In Emilia's the things bought in Rio and in the shop on board don't fit; when she tries to put them in my suitcase, I say to her: "Please, don't put anything in mine. I'm not going home." "Where are you going?" "To a hotel." "What are you telling me?" "That I'm not going home." "Why?" "Because I'm leaving. I already telegraphed Doctor Sivori." This announcement affects

her more than I could have foreseen. She gets so pale that I'm alarmed. She doesn't blink an eye, but opens her eyes wide, and her mouth. Before I can prevent it, she throws herself at my feet, kisses them, and repeats without interruption: "I'll never be bad again. Forgive me. I'll never be bad again. Forgive me." . . . To calm her down, I take her in my arms and, before I know it, we're in bed making love. Then she resumes her tears and the request to forgive her. I agree to forgive her and to telegraph Sivori ("We made up"). Emilia whispers in my ear: "For those who love one another, there's nothing that can't be fixed between the sheets." Seeing her so content, I believe myself to be happy.

EPILOGUE

Without thinking much about it I went off to the apartment on Chilavert Street, which my friend rented after the second breakup. As there was nobody in the entrance and upstairs they didn't open the door for me, I figured that it wasn't there. I had to search a while, to find the superintendent. "No," the man confirmed, "it's not here," and he continued talking to some electricians. Before I could ask him anything, he disappeared with the electricians down a staircase that led to the basement.

I didn't know what to do. From a public telephone I called Mileo. He said to me: "He's in her house. That's why I'm not going." I answer him: "I am, though I understand you perfectly."

His wife's house is in Palermo Chico. Upon entering, I almost say out loud: "What a sad wake." An absurd thought. The wife and some female relatives or friends were having a lively conversation. They were silent upon seeing me; the wife sobbed. I only remember that I crossed the room to say goodby to Lucio. Poor man. It seemed to me he was resting at ease, in his coffin.

F.B.

Underwater

When I finally got over the hepatitis, the doctor recommended I go away for a few days to the mountains, the coast, or the country, to any place where I could take it easy and breathe fresh air. I picked up the telephone and announced to Señora Pons that I wouldn't have the deed done until May 20th. Thompson said to me:

"But, Martelli, why are you committing yourself to be here at a set date? I'll take care of the deed . . ."

"You know how it is. Señora . . ."

"From your bouquet of exclusive old ladies?"

Among the clientele of the Thompson and Martelli Notary Service are a bunch of ladies who trust only me.

"I'll be back on the 20th. Meanwhile I'll see how it goes."

"If you're not afraid of solitude, you could go to my house on Lake Quillén, quite a beautiful place. You won't go hungry because the housekeeper, a Señora Fredrich, has a flair for cooking. What I regret is not being able to go with you."

"A lake in the South!" I exclaimed. "It must be marvelous! But, forgive me if I'm obsessive: Is there any fishing there?"

"Several kinds of salmon, steelhead trout, even mackerel . . ."

Late in the afternoon, a little before sundown, I reached Quillén. I felt tired, a little weak and cold. The Andes, the lake, the forest, the lush green vegetation, put me in a state of joyous self-communion; but the cool air, despite all my clothes, gave me the chills, so that I quickly knocked on the door of a house (the only one in sight) made of logs and which seemed to be right in the lake. A woman peered out, with her hair parted in the middle, and with bulging breasts. She said imperturbably:

"Aldo Martelli the notary public? I was expecting you."

We entered a large room, where the fire was lit. I went directly to the fireplace and stretched out my open hands. I would have gladly continued watching the logs burn, but the woman asked:

"Shall I take your suitcase to the room?"

I told her not to bother, grabbed my suitcase, and followed the woman. Upon seeing in my room a puma-skin rug beside the bed, a desk, a window facing the lake, I said to myself: "I'm going to do just fine." I went over to the window, looked out at the scenery and, as I felt a bit cold, returned to the living room. After a while the woman served me an excellent meal, which revived me. I still remember our conversation. I said to her:

"From the window of my room one can see, over the

lake, a bit far away, a log cabin similar to this, but with a top floor. It's inhabited, or at least smoke is coming out of the chimney. Who lives there?"

"Doctor Salmon," she answered.

"Excellent news. A doctor at hand is always comforting. A rural doctor, better yet, because instead of ordering x-rays and lab tests, he actually cures people."

"This one is considered eminent," the woman paused, "but as far as practicing medicine goes, he doesn't have a practice."

"There are few people in the area."

"That's not the reason. For this doctor people don't count. Salmon count."

I hurried to respond:

"For me too. Is there any fishing?"

"Of course, and a motorboat."

After a while I went to bed, because sleep was closing my eyes. Already in bed, I wondered if I had enough blankets. I thought I did, that it wasn't worth the trouble to look for the woman to give me a reinforcement. I waited gradually for my body to get warm. This occurred, though not in as definite a way as I wished. I wondered if that slight lack of heat wouldn't end up giving me a cold and the flu. I also wondered: "Could going so far away from civilization, after my illness, be a serious mistake? Places like this are for young people, with iron constitutions." Of course, Señora Fredrich was not at all young, but it was one thing to be a newcomer and another to be an inhabitant who had always been there. "What a mistake to die in Quillén."

These broodings kept me awake: To tell the truth, I

still wonder if I stayed awake because I was thinking or if I was thinking because the cold—moderate, it's true, but without a doubt cold—was not allowing me to get to sleep.

The next day, when I woke up, I was still not warm; I continued to feel tired, but miraculously I wasn't sick. In order not to get sick, I spent the whole day beside the fire.

At night, in my bed, I said to myself: "Frankly, this marvelous place is not for me. After the endless solitude of hepatitis, I come all the way here, to be alone. Without a kindred spirit to talk to, I'm paying too much attention to myself, discovering alarming symptoms, predicting illnesses, getting sick. I must be one of those persons who, if they're not surrounded by people, fade away and die."

I thought too that in order to sleep at night, I should tire myself out during the day. If I took the road that went along the lake, I would have as the goal of my walks Doctor Salmon's house. This would be at first an unreachable goal, but I would go that far as soon as I recovered my strength. The road itself, between the unfolding beauty of the lake on the right, and the trees on my left, would be the best stimulation to keep walking.

From the second morning on I faithfully followed my plan of daily walks. Except for an Indian here and there, offering squash or ponchos in exchange for tobacco, *yerba maté,* or sugar, and some kids in smocks hurrying off to school, I never met up with anybody, until the afternoon I noticed a woman sitting on the steps going down to the lake, on the dock of the doctor's house. As I drew near, I saw that she was a redhead; she had sports clothes on, loose and white; her hands were crossed on her knee; she was very beautiful.

Without much effort, I reached the doctor's house. The woman, who seemed distracted in her contemplation of the water, suddenly stood, and ran up the steps. I didn't dare to detain her with a shout, but I watched her disappear into the house. Why had she left so hastily? I wasn't sure if she had seen me. In any case, at no moment had she looked in my direction.

To ease my doubt, expecially to see the woman, I would knock on the door. I immediately reconsidered: if for any reason she didn't want to see me, introducing myself to her would be a mistake. Nobody likes to be forced. It would be better for me to leave; with a little luck I would awaken her curiosity.

I spent the whole afternoon thinking about the unknown woman. I told myself that I was behaving like a silly little boy and that perhaps hepatitis had brought me back to youth, or more probably, my second childhood. Why was I so agitated? As if I had seen a goddess! "As far as I know," I said, speaking to myself, "the only extraordinary being in this region is the plesiosaurus."

Fortunately I managed to get a hold of myself. If I'm remembering correctly, at nightfall, I was reading old magazines and, after a pleasant dinner, I fell fast asleep. I won't deny, however, that the next morning my first impulse was to run to the window and look at the doctor's house. I regretted not having binoculars.

After breakfast I started out on the walk with my thoughts focused on the woman. Playing a game I didn't believe in, mentally I called her. It didn't take me long to see, in the distance, something that seemed extraordinary to me: the unknown woman coming out of the house and taking the path that led her to me.

A while later, when we met up, she smiled, and something in her attitude made me feel that there was some sort of an agreement between us. She told me her name was Flora Guibert; by way of an explanation she added that she was the niece of Professor Guibert. I said:

"I'm Aldo Martelli the notary public. I'm staying at the house of my partner, Thompson."

Thinking that good sense counseled me to hide my desire to draw out the conversation and detain Flora, I noticed that she did not hide a similar desire. I felt like inviting her to have lunch at home with me, but I abstained because when men rush into things they annoy women. Flora asked me:

"Shall we see each other tomorrow?"

"Let's see each other," I said.

"Around nine, right here?"

"Right here."

The rest of the day I was happy, but anxious. The next morning I regretted that the date wasn't for a little later, because there's nothing worse than bathing and having breakfast with just enough time. When I went out I asked Señora Fredrich if she would mind if I invited Doctor Guibert's niece to lunch.

"Why should I mind?" she asked. "I practically saw her mother give birth to her. Her name is Flora."

I felt affection for Señora Fredrich and even an impulse to thank her for having pronounced the name of my new friend.

In order to continue talking about her I observed:

"She's a very pleasant person."

What I heard next I didn't like.

"A very fine girl, and so well-mannered! But, believe me, she's not what one would call lucky. Just to tell you that she's been going out with a man more than twenty years older than her. A bum without a university degree."

For a few seconds, as Señora Fredrich spoke, I feared that she had found out—don't ask me how—about our meeting and that the bum in question was myself. Regarding the age factor, I said to myself that as young as Flora seemed, I couldn't be more than ten or fifteen years older than her.

I started out on the road, with a superstitious fear. By being so certain that we were going to meet, perhaps I wouldn't see her that afternoon, or ever again. I was still trying to get out of my head this bad omen, when I thought I saw her among the trees, which in that place form a very thick grove. I wasn't wrong: there was Flora, hidden among twining branches, sitting on the ground, leaning against a tree, prettier than in my memory. She extended a hand toward me and moving her forefinger called to me. I said:

"How awful it would have been if I had passed you by."

With displeasure I thought that my exclamation sounded like a reproach.

"I saw you," she answered.

I had at the moment the conviction that everything—
the woman's beauty, the silence of the place, contem-
plating the forest—all came together to suggest to me the
idea of embracing her immediately. Of course, I didn't
know how to proceed. Meanwhile Flora, in an almost
imperceptible way at first, moved away from the tree, lay
down face up, and stretched out her arms to me. Totally
giddy I reflected that I should contain my excitement,
because nothing is more unpleasant than the awkward
advances of a man beside himself; but I immediately
realized that Flora also had a great desire to embrace
me.

Afterward I invited her to lunch. I told her she could
be sure that at that very moment, Señora Fredrich was
cooking great delicacies in the kitchen, because she loved
her and was looking forward to seeing her.

"I love her too," she answered. "Let's go, but first let's
go by the house, because I have to let my uncle know
that I'm not having lunch with him."

"Let's go," I said. "Señora Fredrich doesn't like people to arrive late at her table."

We entered Doctor Guibert's house. Flora made me
go into a little room filled with books, indicated a chair,
and said:

"I'll be back in a minute."

On the wall opposite me there was a painting. I looked
at it without curiosity. It consisted of a wide red vertical
stripe that opened like a *y* into two thinner, oblique
stripes, with red and white veins. I thought: "Even I, if I
set myself to it, could do a painting like this."

Where Flora had gone out, a short while later a man in

a white smock came in. He was quite old, with a ruddy face, blue eyes, and trembling hands. He asked:

"Martelli, I presume?"

"Doctor Guibert?"

"Florita spoke to me about you. Do you like the region? Not as much as I do, I'll bet!"

"I like it a lot."

"Are you going to stay a while?"

"A few days. I came to recuperate . . ."

"Don't tell me you're sick."

"I was."

"And here I imagined you to be brimming with health! What was the matter?"

"Hepatitis."

"Almost nothing. Any repercussions? I'll bet you're not the same man you were."

Annoyed I replied:

"I'm perfectly fine." Upon seeing that his hands trembled, I gave myself the pleasure of adding: "And—what not everybody can say—free of Parkinson's."

"What made you come to Lake Quillén?"

"My friend Thompson offered me the house. I wanted to breathe fresh air and be free of worries."

"Say, rather, to have different worries. Or didn't you know that wherever one goes, one finds them?"

I thought that as old and wise as he was he didn't have to treat me with that superior tone. To pay him back in the same coin, I pointed to the painting and asked:

"Where did you get that thing of beauty?"

With a smile he answered:

"I too don't understand a thing about painting. It's a 'Phoenix' by Randazzo:"

"A what?"

"A painting by Willi Randazzo. A rather well-known painter and, besides, a friend of Florita's. But here she is!"

The girl announced to him:

"I'm going to lunch with Martelli."

Putting a hand on my shoulder, Guibert said:

"You're taking away my niece. Take good care of her. She's a wonderful person."

I agreed with this last remark, and the request moved me. I thought: "I'd better be careful. I like this girl too much." When we left the house, Flora took me by the hand and made me run. She said:

"Let's take the path behind the trees. That way is as pretty as along the lake."

"But it takes more time," I said to myself.

We didn't get there late. Señora Fredrich received Flora with great displays of joy and affection, which were brief because her real concern was not to overcook the meal. Every meal at Señora Fredrich's is unique, incites praise, and leaves one in a good mood.

When she left the room, we kissed beside the fireplace. I took my friend by the hand and led her to my bedroom. As in the forest I embraced her so eagerly that I thought: "I should control myself. I must seem crazy." But it didn't take long for me to notice that the eagerness with which Flora embraced me was so extreme that I wondered if I shouldn't be wary, because all excess in the long run is bad for the health.

Around four in the afternoon, Flora said that she had to go. We ran into Señora Fredrich in the living room, and Flora started chatting with her. As I had the intention of taking her home, I thought that perhaps it might get cool and that I'd better take a scarf for my neck. I went to get it in my room and there, on the hanger, was my overcoat. In a second fit of prudence I put it on, and then I overheard, unintentionally, the women's conversation.

"Is everything the same with Randazzo?" the lady asked.

Flora answered:

"The same, no."

"But it still goes on?"

"I don't know. I don't know anything. I feel confused."

"Poor thing."

I am very jealous. I'm not exaggerating: my blood froze. My heart palpitated noticeably. As I feared she would notice my state of shock, I leaned against the door and, before leaving my room, counted to ten.

Señora Fredrich accompanied us through the garden and opened the gate. We had barely gone three or four steps, when Flora exclaimed:

"Now I know how much I love you," to communicate to me immediately in an uplifted and triumphant tone: "You're going to take me along the lake."

"Good," I responded, with a little voice that seemed unpleasant to me.

She took me firmly by the waist and made me run beside her.

"Don't go thinking that I'm in a hurry to get there. I'm running because I'm happy."

"It's getting late," I indicated.

Flora didn't hear, or didn't pay any attention. She said:

"What a wonderful day. I loved you among the trees, and I loved you more after lunch."

The idea that Flora had another man disturbed me, and that she was so pretty provoked despair. I must be too sensitive, too frank. I told myself that if I was anxious to clear things up, perhaps the most expeditious way would be to ask for an explanation. I would run the risk, of course, of irritating her and of forcing her to lie to me. But I shouldn't give her any warning, if I wanted to discover the truth.

"Is something wrong?" she asked.

"I'm not feeling well," I answered.

Again that unpleasant and hypocritical little voice came out.

"If you're not well, don't take me home. I always walk alone here. I should recommend you not to get too close to the edge of the lake. It's dangerous."

I thought: "She must think my health is bad and that I'm going to lose my balance and fall into the water." I almost explained the truth to her. I was very offended that she didn't understand it was all her fault.

I thought that as soon as I left her I would feel calm. I was wrong. As soon as I was alone, I felt vexed and anxious. Luckily Señora Fredrich served me tea with scones, toast, and raspberry jam. I ate copiously and recovered my sense of well-being. The two acts of love today must have had some part in this. After a long abstinence, physical love is invigorating. Repeating it was perhaps an excess; I would be more cautious the next time.

From Flora I would receive whatever good she gave me, without compromising my soul. I think I said to myself: "There's obviously no lack of proof that she's an easy woman; from easy to promiscuous is a short step . . . I must protect myself, because I'm very sensitive and I don't want to suffer."

I spent the last hours of the afternoon with a book, beside the fireplace. After an exquisite dinner, which I accorded its due praise, I slept till the next day.

I awoke in an admirable mood and in a better physical state. I would repress my desire to see Flora, as well as my impatience to find out the truth about my rival. To achieve both things, I would literally follow her recommendation; in my walks I would avoid the edge of the lake; I would go in the opposite direction, till reaching the town. In the afternoon, in the boat, I would give myself the joy of fishing. In any case I considered the day ahead as a hard experiment, which I hoped to come out of stronger. What I would have given to see Flora immediately!

The morning walk was tolerable. The people in the area seemed quite pleasant. I bought, in town, a poncho woven by the Indians and the Nuns' Liqueur which—according to my experience on more than one occasion—cured stomach aches, frequent in gluttonous men like myself. I always try to have a little bottle on hand in my medicine chest.

During lunch Señora Fredrich did not talk about Flora and, for my part, I restrained from mentioning her so as not to appear anxious. I would have liked her to tell me that at some moment in the morning my new girlfriend had come to the house to ask for me. The mere idea of having to spend the whole afternoon and night before being with her again provoked in me a faint feeling; but I thought that I shouldn't falter, if I wanted the sacrifice of not seeing her to serve for something.

As I prepared bait and flies, I remembered a phrase that I often say to whoever wishes to hear me: for me there's no greater paradise than an afternoon spent fishing. I'm not being untruthful, however, if I confess that upon starting up the motorboat, I felt more resignation than expectations: In reality everything that meant not seeing Flora irritated me like an unforgivable waste of time.

I let the line out, so as to drag the fly far from the boat: I advanced very slowly, so that the noise of the motor wouldn't frighten the fish. As soon as I reached the middle of the lake, the boat began to rock as if, from below, some monstrous animal were shaking it, determined to throw me into the water. I managed to grab hold of the accelerator: with one big push the boat freed itself. I looked backward, for fear of being chased. I saw for a moment, or thought I saw, in the white wake, a bloodstain. Even though I was going at top speed, the way back to the dock seemed endless to me. From firm ground I cast a glance at the lake, which was as serene as ever, and entered the house. I can state that I had to close the door to feel secure. Señora Fredrich reassuringly exclaimed:

"You came back soon. One gets bored fishing."

"I don't, but I had the fright of my life."

"The boat had a leak?"

"Not even a drop, but it began to rock. I don't know what animal it must have been: I swear, if I hadn't sped away, it would have turned me over."

"Don't worry about it. The only time I went out fishing the same thing happened to me."

"Something tried to capsize your boat?"

"In the middle of the lake I was afraid. I wanted to come back as soon as possible."

"They didn't shake your boat?"

"No, but I was afraid all the same."

"I'm going to my room, to read a little."

"Read something nice, to clear your head . . ."

I think she said: "Of those things you dreamed." I know when I'm about to have a fit of temper, and I also know it's not good for the health, so without answering I went to my room.

The following day dawned rainy and cold. As the bad weather lasted through the night, I stayed at home all day, so as not to run any risks.

The next morning I went out for a walk. It's curious: two days of inactivity had been enough to make me lose the endurance gained on my previous walks. I had not gone more than halfway when I had to sit down, on a rock, to rest.

I looked at the lake. Suddenly I thought I saw, under

the water, a long body, perhaps pink, which didn't give me time to fix my attention upon it, and it disappeared into the deep, like an iridescent reflection. It could be an animal, or a swimmer; but as it did not come up to the surface, I said to myself that it must be an animal . . . A monster from the lake that moved like a swimming man. Another hypothesis: a corpse carried by currents in those deep waters. I thought: "It's possible that there are currents, because this lake connects, who knows how, with the Pacific Ocean. Maybe it was a fisherman who had been less lucky than I. Or, perhaps, the monster that almost capsized my boat." I then remembered that Flora had warned me not to go near the lake. I immediately stood up, took a few steps back while reaching the conclusion that if the animal were marauding around, he was doing so in the hopes of catching me.

I continued on my way, rehearsing the conversation I'd have with Flora about this animal I saw, or thought I saw, when it seemed to me that something, colored white, was moving in the water. Curiosity won over prudence; I approached the shore. I glimpsed—how shall I say?—a white body, or perhaps an object moving away, and which I interpreted as a fox terrier, or even more absurdly, as a lamb. I stood waiting for it to come up to breathe. Very soon it disappeared from sight.

As soon as I reached the house, Flora made me come in and took me to the little book-filled room of former times. There she indicated to me the chair facing the painting, which struck me as a bad omen.

She seemed calm, a little distant. I hadn't been concerned by the possibility of finding her thus, in the previous forty-eight hours, but now I would have given anything to feel her affectionate and joyous. My jealousy and the shame of confessing it had led me to strategies that displeased her. The poor thing, at the beginning, believed blindly in our love, but she didn't fool herself in interpreting my absence and was now rather bitterly disillusioned. If I had acknowledged that I acted out of jealousy, perhaps she would have forgiven me: vanity prevented such a confession. Flora said:

"Before meeting you, I was in love with another man. Maybe out of cowardice I didn't dare follow him. When I saw you I was sure of finding true love, unquestionable love, you understand?"

"Of course I understand. I felt the same."

"I thought with you I could forget Willie."

"Willie? Who's Willie?"

I almost said: "Who the hell is Willie?" Flora answered:

"Randazzo. The great painter."

The words "the great painter" seemed to me the first foolish thing I had heard her say. This sign that she was not a person free of faults did not make me love her less. On the contrary, it provoked tenderness and allowed me to adopt the always satisfying role of protector.

"So you couldn't forget this Willie?" I asked.

"No, I couldn't. Perhaps you weren't too much of a help . . . The day before yesterday, in the morning, you didn't come see me, and in the afternoon you went out fishing."

"I like fishing . . ."

"That's obvious. Then the next day . . ."

"It was cold, it snowed. That's why I stayed home."

"Okay . . . I'm only asking that you try to understand. In order to leave Willie, I needed you to love me a lot."

"I do love you a lot."

"I know, but not enough. Please, don't jump to conclusions . . ."

"Why would I?"

"Because I told you that I didn't dare follow Willie. Don't think he's a bad person. He's violent, perhaps, but very loyal and, deep down, understanding."

Each time Flora said "Willie," I was irritated.

"A beautiful person but so as not to go with him you grabbed onto the first fool . . ."

"Don't talk like that . . . Of course if I don't explain it to you, you're not going to understand. Did you remember not to go near the lake?"

I don't know why I didn't want to mention the white dog, or rather the lamb. I answered:

"Sort of. But before you told me anything I had a terrible experience."

I told her about the boat incident. She got seriously alarmed; how different from Señora Fredrich: she believed me, she wasn't coming out with irritating interpretations. I thought: "This woman loves me." As I didn't have much more to say and she was asking me for details, I continued with what I saw in the water when I sat down to rest. Worried, Flora reminded me:

"I told you to avoid going near."

Maybe I thought that if I awakened her compassion, she would love me again. I asked:

"If you're going to leave me, why should I take care of myself?"

I said this like an actor, like a swindler who cares only about achieving his goal. I didn't think she would get so sad. When she looked at my eyes, hers, which are beautiful, expressed alarm and pain. I felt almost ashamed. Flora said that she would explain everything to me, because she was sure that if she requested it of me, I wouldn't speak about these things. I agreed. She then observed:

"For me it's a great responsibility, because I didn't consult my uncle."

I was about to ask her what Doctor Guibert had to do with our matter, but she didn't give me any time and began the explanation.

She said that she had always been the assistant at Doctor Guibert's laboratory, except for one period, at the end of last year. As if it were the most natural thing in the world she told me that she then went to Buenos Aires, for a week, with Randazzo, and that the week stretched out into four months. When she returned she feared that Guibert would reproach her for her long delay. He didn't, nor did he ask her how it had gone. The old man, with a radiant face and arms akimbo, exclaimed:

"I have good news. Either I'm very wrong or I have found the fountain of youth."

"Where?"

His response was surprising:

"In the salmon."

It was as if I had been hit over the head with a bat. From the moment Flora had said that she had spent a season with that man I felt my head going around in circles, and I only half listened; when she mentioned the salmon, I perked up. And a good thing, too, because what Flora said right then is essential in order to understand the whole matter: in salmon there's a gland that rejuvenates them when they're about to undertake their sea voyage. The gland functions only once. It functions so that they undertake their odyssey in the flower of youth. She explained:

"If instead of being a salmon it were a man, the gland would return him to his youth of twenty years of age."

I do not know why the heck I started arguing and insisting that the best moment of a man's life was after his thirties and perhaps after his forties. As she didn't respond, I tried a question:

"When the salmon is old, does he return to die in his native river or lake?"

"Of course, but that's not relevant," she said and continued the explanation.

Grafting the gland of a fish on organisms of other species presented difficulties that were overcome. Flora said she listened very attentively to her uncle's explanations and then commented on them with Randazzo. Some time before, Randazzo had told her: "The luck of finding you came along with the misfortune of turning sixty." Upon finding out about Guibert's research, he asked Flora to put him on the "waiting list of guinea pigs." As regards Guibert, at the beginning, he contended that the margin of safety in his procedure still did not permit experiments with human beings. In any case, since Randazzo's eagerness to be rejuvenated was no greater than Guibert's to try it out, Guibert let himself be convinced, though he predicted that the newly implanted gland would not produce rejuvenation, that this would take some time, as in the salmon . . . "If I understood correctly," Randazzo had said, "the salmon is not rejuvenated until he goes out to sea." "No, it's the other way around: the salmon does not go out to sea until he's rejuvenated. He undertakes the great adventure when he feels the revival of his youth. For your own peace of mind, remember that all salmon go out to sea. That is, the gland never fails."

Flora mentioned that in her uncle's laboratory, in the same house where we were talking, they grafted onto Randazzo four glands, because the human body is bigger than the salmon's. His body showed no signs of rejection. The man recovered and so well that uncle and niece soon believed they could detect symptoms of an incipient rejuvenation. A few days later, however, a respiratory complication and a kind of irritation in the skin developed. Randazzo had repeated and increasing attacks of suffocation. Guibert took an x-ray of his thorax which revealed the lungs to be severely diminished. Despite vasodilating remedies, the affliction grew worse. Regarding his skin, what there was were scales.

A few days later, in a second x-ray, the lungs seemed withered. Flora thought she saw the appearance of other new ones. This revived her hopes, but Randazzo started choking. Doctor Guibert acted. Before Flora's shocked eyes and without saying a word, he took him to the edge of the lake, gave him a push and, now in the water, took his head and held it under. Flora tried to rescue her lover, but in surprise she saw him swimming underwater. What she had taken for new lungs were gills. Every few minutes Randazzo emerged from the water, holding his nose, and with a muffled voice shouting: "I'll never forgive what you did to me." "You're going to pay for this." "Either you send me Flora or I'll kill you."

She did not resign herself to leaving him in the water and had a long conversation with him, which fatigued him noticeably. When Flora said to him: "My uncle couldn't know that instead of lungs you would have gills," Randazzo repeatedly came up to shout: "He knew, he knew. He had experimented with animals." Flora asked him if he was cold; it seems that in the first moments yes, but that he soon got used to it. "Do you remember that I was getting scales on my skin? Now all I have is scales! I assure you that if some day I come out of the lake, your uncle's only hope is to disappear off the face of the earth." "Physically I'm not suffering," Randazzo said, "but I don't see how I'm going to resign myself to not painting." This consequence, which greatly moved Flora, for some reason made me feel like laughing. It seems that one of most permanent causes of Randazzo's fury was my relationship with Flora. He said that he would do nothing to her, but that he would kill Guibert and me. Why me, who barely knew of his existence, who never had any intention of harming him and who, if I stole Flora's love, was obeying the laws of

nature, which don't depend on our will power? Flora
made him see that if he killed her uncle, she could never
be reunited with him. "The day you come to the lake, I'll
forgive him, I swear." He dived into the water; when he
came up again he shouted: "The other one I'll never
forgive." He went down again; he came out again ardu-
ously, to shout what had already been heard: "I'll never
forgive." Why deny it? I was glad that the pest was
where he was.

According to Flora, Randazzo did not doubt that she
would convince Guibert to operate on her.

"He believes in my love," she said, shaking her head,
and I was about to believe that at the last moment she
silenced the words, "Not like others." She continued
saying: "And the worst is that I doubted at the beginning. Everything frightened me. The coldness of the lake
and the change of life style. Living among animals I hate.
I don't like fish."

When the rejuvenation happened to Randazzo, would
she have to accompany him on the excursion to the sea?
The idea frightened her. Nevertheless, she spoke to her
uncle, to convince him to graft the glands onto her. At
the beginning he didn't want to listen to her. He exclaimed: "How could Randazzo possibly think that I
would salmonize my most beloved niece? Because of
your age the grafting doesn't make any sense, and the
experiment is still not sufficiently proven. When I operated on Randazzo I didn't know that the gland had those
effects on the respiratory system. Committing a mistake
like that once is unforgivable. The second time it
wouldn't be a mistake."

In a fit of curiosity I asked Flora what Randazzo ate. She immediately answered:

"I suppose smaller fish."

She blushed and explained that at the beginning they gave him normal food, which turned out to be a strain because it scattered in the water. The food for fish was well received, but came in insufficient amounts. Perhaps because of this Randazzo, who soon got impatient, one day told her not to bother to bring him more food. "From then on, the poor thing had to imitate the practices of the other inhabitants of the lake."

Flora maintained that Randazzo was a strong man who always managed to do what he set out to do. She next confessed to me that the day we met she bet on me, like a gambler who places all his chips, all his fortune, on a number. The number did not come up.

"I don't blame you," she said. "I grabbed onto you as onto a lifesaver. I thought that destiny had sent you to me, that there was a great affinity between us."

"There is," I protested.

"Up to a certain point . . . My aspiration was a little absurd. I wanted to find the love of my life, a love that would allow me, without remorse, to leave Randazzo in that world that is now his, so different from ours."

She said that my behavior provoked in her a painful but definitely desirable awakening. It was obvious to her that I didn't love her like Randazzo.

I asked her why Randazzo had tried to capsize my boat.

"Because he saw you with me. Because he is jealous

like you, but very violent. He says, besides, that you hurt his arm with the propeller."

"He wanted to knock my boat over. He must have the instinctive ferocity of the creatures that live underwater."

"Not at all. If he knows that someone has acted well, he's capable of setting aside any resentment. He's very noble and very understanding. I assure you that if my uncle operates on me, Willie will forgive him. Exactly as I said, he'll forgive him."

At this point, Flora dispensed with a certain minimal but irreducible harshness, with which she had been treating me till then, and upon continuing her line of reasoning she declared that if I loved her as I affirmed, Guibert could operate on both of us. It was with tremendous surprise that I heard those words.

"Operate on us?" I asked.

"If you believe in me a little (I didn't fail you) you must believe in what I'm telling you: the three of us can live in harmony, because Randazzo loves me enough to share me with another person."

I won't deny that my first reaction was one of authentic alarm. Instinctively I hid it but acted upon the heartfelt conviction that I should, above all, hold on with tooth and nail to this world of ours, not to let myself be dragged down to that other mysterious and threatening one, where the wretched Randazzo was. In the second place, but with no less determination, I should hold onto Flora. I regarded with skepticism the probability of Randazzo's tolerating me. Flora said that she knew him better than I did. I then asked that we put off our operation a little, since I would be going on the 19th to Buenos Aires, to notarize a deed for my old client Señora Pons. I insisted that I wouldn't be there for more than two days. Flora's reaction was curious. The excuse—because that's how she took my words, as an excuse—seemed comical to her, and I don't exactly understand why. It also made her sad, which did seem comprehensible, because a separation is always painful. As she wasn't convinced by anything I said, I resorted to the argument that no matter how much Randazzo reconciled himself to it, I would never reconcile myself to sharing her. As I stated this, I was afraid Flora would say to me: "Then your affection for me is less than his," but she didn't say that and, amazingly, she seemed moved. Life is a game of chess, and one never knows for certain when you're winning or losing. I thought I had scored a point in my favor. I had, but I had also taken a step closer to danger. In effect, Flora told me to get hold of myself, that I shouldn't let jealousy prevent us from living together, and that the idea of sharing her, as intolerable as it now seemed to me, in time would be tolerable, and then the three of us would really achieve happiness.

"There might be an obstacle," I hurried to say. "Who knows if your uncle will agree . . ."

"How could you think that?" she asked, adding in a jollier tone: "My uncle can't wait to have more guinea pigs."

"You might be right. At the beginning, the day we met, he seemed very interested in me, but when he found out that I had been sick, he almost got mad. He must have thought I wouldn't be useful to him."

"How could you think that. You're stronger than anybody."

"How do I know. Maybe those who have had hepatitis are no good for the operation."

"I assure you that nobody will object to your operation. My poor uncle. I'm his only volunteer and, if he sends me to the lake, he'll be left alone. But you'll soon see that I'll convince him. Since he doesn't like Randazzo, he'll be very happy to send you with me to the lake."

She took me by the hand, led me to her room, and we went to bed. At first I was a little worried by the possibility that Guibert would suddenly appear, but Flora was so focused on what we were doing that I continued her example. Women lead us, and we men follow.

Our separation was heartrending. Again she loved me as before, but accepted with reservations my promises to return soon. Because of that incredulity, I almost didn't dare remind her of the second promise, that of allowing Guibert to operate on me. "In all this," I thought, "I should see the proof of love that Flora gives me. She loves me even though she doesn't believe my words. So different from me."

In Buenos Aires, at the beginning, everything was accomplished as planned. Thompson seemed proud of my enthusiasm for the Quillén region, and agreed that I should return as soon as possible, to prolong my rest period a little. Señora Pons signed the deed. The following day, when I asked for Thompson, I was told: "He announced he's not coming." "Yesterday I thought he had quite a cold," I commented. I called him at home. He said that he had the flu, but that in twenty-four hours he would be back in the office. He had a high fever and didn't return for over a week; I had no choice but to put off my return to Quillén. I had to stand in for my partner on two documents. The secretary, who is not particularly friendly with me, gave me the satisfaction of commenting: "I always say, you are irreplaceable at Thompson and Martelli." I admit that I thought: "She's right." I also thought: "This postponement of my return, which I haven't sought out, causes me a little anguish, but perhaps I should give Flora some time to think things over and discard an idea which continues to seem so absurd, so unpleasant."

When I finally reached Lake Quillén—one evening a little before sundown—Señora Fredrich received me like an old friend. I asked:

"Any news?"

"None. Everything's the same."

"Has Flora visited you?"

She said no. I said to myself, bitterly, that my delay obviously didn't disturb her too much, since she didn't even bother to ask for news. It's curious: it took me a while to realize that I was the one at fault. When I understood it, I wanted at all costs to avoid delaying any longer. I almost went off to Doctor Guibert's house, but night, the cold, the snow dissuaded me. I looked out the window and didn't see any lights. Either the night was very dark or the doctor and his niece had gone to bed early.

Between the effect of the copious meal and my fatigue, I overslept. No sooner did I awake than I ran to the window. With distress I noticed that no smoke was coming out of the chimney at the Guibert house. This, added to the lack of lights on the previous night, alarmed me. "What a disaster," I said to myself, "if I have come back here, to discover that Flora and her uncle went to Buenos Aires. And if I go back to Buenos Aires, how do I find them?"

After a frugal breakfast I walked to Guibert's house, staying, of course, far from the shore. How many wonderful memories were evoked by this walk. How close, and yet, how far they now were. I arrived finally and knocked on the door. Nobody answered. I tried to open. I couldn't. I tried one window after the next, and when I was already starting to get desperate, one yielded to the pressure of my hand.

On the desk I found a letter. It said:

"Dear Aldo: My uncle operated on me. Unfortunately you won't be able to be operated on, because Willie, when I was in bed, recovering from the operation, thought that he had sent me to Buenos Aires with you and, at a moment when my uncle was on the steps of the dock, like a water spout he shot up and they had an agitated argument. My poor uncle lost his balance and drowned in the lake. But don't worry about me. I assure you that despite my pain, for him and for you, I'm happy that he operated on me before drowning. Now I have to enter the lake because I'm beginning to feel the choking. Forgive me for not waiting for you. Love always, your Flora."

Desolate, I realized that my behavior had been absurd: losing Flora over a client's deed! I deserved the worst punishment, even though, to tell the truth, I don't think that anybody accepts, just like that, such a strange plan as the one Flora proposed to me. Of course, if instead of fulfilling, like a robot, my notary duties, I had stayed with the only person who mattered to me, I would have prevented her operation or, as a last resort, I would have asked Guibert to operate on me too and now I would be with her, in the lake, in the sea, at the end of the world. "Why did I stay so many days in Buenos Aires?" I said to myself disconsolately. "If I had come back on the promised date I would have prevented this madness, this veritable suicide." Like a sleepwalker I left the room, reached the edge of the steps to the dock. It took only a moment for me to notice Flora and Randazzo close together, underwater, who smiled at me and waved their hands in a repeated greeting, apparently happy.

Three Fantasies
in Minor Key

MARGARITA OR
THE POWER OF PHARMACEUTICALS

"Your success, poor brief success"
from Holding Hands (*a tango*)

I don't remember why my son reproached me on a certain occasion:

"Everything always goes so smoothly for you."

He lived at home, with his wife and four children, the oldest an eleven-year-old boy, the youngest a two-year-old named Margarita. Since these words revealed resentment, I was concerned. At one point I brought up the subject with my daughter-in-law, saying:

"You won't deny that there's something repellent about success."

"Success is the natural result of work well done," she replied.

"It always involves some vanity, some vulgarity."

"Not success," she interrupted me, "but rather the desire for success. Condemning success seems excessively romantic to me, no doubt convenient for bunglers."

114

Despite her intelligence, my daughter-in-law did not manage to convince me. Searching for the source of my guilt I looked back on my life, which I have spent between chemistry books and a laboratory of pharmaceutical products. My successes, if there were any, have been authentic perhaps, but not spectacular. In what could be called a career paved with honors, I've come to be the head of the laboratory. I have my own house and a good income. It's true that some formulas of mine resulted in balms, ointments, and tinctures which are displayed on the shelf of every drugstore in our vast country and which, according to hearsay, have relieved more than a few ailments. I've allowed myself to doubt such opinions, since the relationship between the specific remedy and the illness always seems rather mysterious to me. Nevertheless, when I conjured up the formula for my tonic Iron Plus, I experienced both the anxiety and certainty of success. I began to brag recklessly that in pharmaceuticals and in medicine—and mark my words, as they say in the pages of the magazine *Faces and Masks*—people consumed an infinite number of tonics and restoratives, until one day vitamins arrived and swept away all those tonics as if they were frauds. The consequences were obvious: vitamins were discredited, inevitably, and in vain the world has returned to the drugstore to relieve weakness and fatigue.

Though it may seem hard to believe, my daughter-in-law was worried about her youngest daughter's lack of appetite. And in fact poor Margarita, with her golden hair and blue eyes, looked languid, pale, sensitive, like a nineteenth-century engraving, the typical little girl who according to tradition or superstition is destined to join the angels at an early age.

My much-celebrated ability to cook up remedies, goaded by the desire to see my granddaughter restored, ran rapidly, and I invented the aforementioned tonic. Its efficiency is prodigious. Four daily spoonfuls were enough to transform Margarita in a few weeks; now brimming with good color, she has grown, indeed filled out, and displays a satisfactory—one might even say disturbingly voracious—appetite. With determination and persistence she seeks her food and, if they don't let her have it, she attacks with fury. This morning at breakfast time, in the dining room, a spectacle awaited me that I won't forget so easily. In the center of the table sat the little girl with a croissant in each hand. I thought I noticed on her blonde doll cheeks a coloration that was too red. She was smeared with jam and blood. The bodies—or remains, rather—of the family rested against one another with their heads together, in a corner of the room. My son, still alive, found the strength to pronounce his last words:

"It's not Margarita's fault."

He said this in the same reproachful tone that he always used with me.

REGARDING A SMELL

On Thursday night Professor Roberto Ravenna sighed several times, but at one in the morning he let out a moan. After reading the last student paper, he had found in the mess on his table a pile with ten more.

A man of an excitable nature, he needed, in order to recover from the day's exhaustion, long nights of sleep; all that week, for various reasons, his nights had been too short. He was very tired. His reading of their monographs revived, as always, his bitterness toward the students. "It's not for nothing," he said. "There are those who don't know a thing, and then there's the guy who knows something but writes in a way that makes you feel like correcting the whole damn thing."

At three-thirty he had finished. He managed to stagger over to the edge of the bed, where he collapsed without taking off his clothes.

Disturbing knocks on the door woke him up. After a moment of confusion, he understood that in order to silence them he had no choice but to get up and go to the door.

"Who's there?" he asked.

"Open up."

"Who's there?"

"Open, open. It's Venancio. Venancio, the clown."

"The one in 6B," Ravenna reflected. In the house, everybody was known by the number of their apartment. Doña Clotilde, the superintendent, named them that way, and under her rule they adopted the code. Without opening he asked:

"What's the matter with you?"

"But what do you mean, 'What's the matter with me,' Doctor Ravenna? The same that's with you and the rest of the building. Don't you smell the odor?"

"Just as long as there's no fire," thought Ravenna, who lived in 7A, the only apartment on the top floor, and he was already imagining himself running downstairs, choking from the smoke. He felt he had no choice but to open the door a crack. Immediately he had to muster all his strength to counter the onslaught by 6B who, using his shoulder as a lever, was trying to force his way in. He fumbled for the latch just in time, and with the other hand held fast to the frame and could recover, by shoving his chest against the door, the inches of his apartment that the clown had invaded. Panting, but with the satisfaction of success, he exclaimed:

"I won't let you in."

"I swear to you, I can't stand the smell any longer. I have to find out where it's coming from."

"I don't smell anything, and let me assure you that there's no fire in my house."

"What fire are you talking about?"

Upon hearing this Ravenna relaxed. He no longer had any worry other than returning to his bed. In an almost friendly tone he said:

"Then you can go and let me sleep. I'm dead tired."

"Without wishing offense, Doctor, do you think I'm stupid?"

The question surprised him since it came from a man who was so polite that when they'd meet in the elevator he could become annoying. Ravenna replied:

"And you, what are you suggesting?"

"According to reliable sources, you, Doctor, teach at the Veterinary School. To be precise, at the Clinic for Small Animals."

"Precisely."

"You haven't brought home some little animal—call it a dog or a cat—in a complete state of putrefaction, have you?"

"You're nuts."

"Are you claiming that the smell comes from no-where?"

"I'll repeat: I don't smell the slightest odor."

"Because you got used to it. When one has a skeleton at home, one soon gets used to the bad smell. I have no doubt that you work on useful experiments for human-ity. But let me come in and take a look around. I promise you, Doctor Ravenna, if I'm wrong, I won't bother you again."

"It would be a fine how-do-you-do for me to let into my house the first lunatic who contends that there's some imaginary smell."

6B answered:

"Don't say 'imaginary' when I can't stand that dis-gusting odor in my nostrils. If I don't find out where it's coming from I'll go crazy."

"Why don't you try Señora Octavia in 6A?"

"You think so? Such a proud lady, a grand dame is more like it; she commands respect. Believe me, Doctor: I wouldn't dare."

"Dare. Maybe you'll get lucky."

He bolted the door and closed the latch. He looked at his watch. "What a disaster," he said. It was five after four in the morning. That night he had slept a quarter of an hour. Though he painfully felt the weight of sleep, curiosity prevailed: trying not to make noise he opened the door again, went out on the landing on tiptoes, went down the staircase until he was halfway down the curve and, against the balustrade, he watched 6B knock on the door of 6A, first timidly, then frenetically. After a while, the lady stuck out her head, which seemed to wear a crown of thorns: they were curlers. 6B hurried to explain:

"It's because of the smell, Madame. The smell coming from here, from your apartment."

The lady pushed him aside with one shove, or punch, in the chest and, before closing the door, exclaimed:

"Some nerve."

Ravenna tiptoed up the steps that he had come down, entered his apartment, closed the door, and threw himself on the bed, with a sensation of relief similar to happiness. At some moment he dreamed of the events that had happened a while before. When he again heard the knocking on his door, he shrewdly thought that he wouldn't pay any attention, because it was all part of a dream; then the violence of the blows awakened him. He said to himself:

"I have to stop that beast before he breaks my door down."

He got out of bed, ran to the door, and upon opening it received a punch in the nose. As he touched it, to make sure it wasn't bleeding, 6B excused himself:

"I didn't mean to hit you, Doctor. I was knocking so that you'd open, and you appeared so suddenly . . ."

"What you really want is for me not to sleep."

"No, no, sir. On that point you are wrong. I want to come in to get out the dead animal."

"What dead animal?" Ravenna asked, who despite, or perhaps because of, the blow was still half-asleep.

"The one that's giving off the smell. I cannot live a minute more with this horrible smell."

"I'm not letting you in. Not under any circumstances."

"Don't force me, Doctor Ravenna; without the least intention I've already hit you once. Let's get rid of the little creature that's rotting away or I won't answer for my actions."

The struggle between the one trying to come in and the one trying to prevent him progressed quickly and violently. The adversaries fell. Several times each one had the other with his back against the floor. On one of these occasions Ravenna bumped his neck and for a few moments was stunned. Without delay 6B stood up. After a rapid perusal of the apartment, he reappeared as Ravenna was rousing himself.

"You were right," said 6B, very sadly. "I didn't find the corpse, Doctor Ravenna, I didn't find it."

"What I'm going to find is my Eibar revolver to shoot you with."

"If you only knew what I'm going through, you wouldn't speak this way. Nobody can live with such an odor in his nasal passages. I swear to you: if you don't rid me of it I'm going to jump out a window."

As Ravenna pushed the intruder out, he said to him:

"Now you want me to take pity on you. You go before I kick you out."

He closed the door, threw himself on the bed, and when the telephone rang, he woke up and saw on the night table that it was eight-thirty. He did not get angry, because the caller was Doctor Garay, his lifelong friend. Though they had followed different careers (Garay was a psychiatrist), they never stopped seeing each other. Garay proposed to him:

"I'll pick you up today at 7:30. We'll sleep at the same lodge, and tomorrow and the next day we'll fish the whole damn day. Okay?"

"Okay. A little calm will be good for me after what's happened."

He related the episodes of the night and comically described the frenzy of 6B over the supposed odor. Garay asked:

"What's 6B's name?"

"Venancio. I think Venancio Aldano."

"From what you've told me and to avoid worse problems, the best thing to do is to come get him."

"Come get him?"

"With an ambulance, to bring him to the Borda Clinic. You relax; I'll take care of him."

There is a boy in every man. In their high school years Garay and Ravenna on more than one occasion had organized practical jokes which became famous. That morning, each one got a good laugh beside his telephone, and they both felt superior to the rest of the world with their witticisms.

The student consultations at the University were unpleasant. Upon hearing their grades they were displeased. Ravenna in turn felt both compassion and fury. He said to himself: "The worst thing is they don't know that they don't know."

He had lunch in a little neighborhood restaurant and without delay went back home: his body was crying out for a siesta. When he was about to get in the elevator, the superintendent came over to him to announce:

"They took 6B to the Borda. Someone must have passed the word. Did you hear the racket he caused last night? For a man like him to behave like that, he must be crazy."

"Twice he woke me up. Do you realize: in the middle of the night he wanted to come into my house."

"He has no sense of decency."

"A total nut. Do you know why he was trying to get in? According to him, I had a dead animal."

"Such madness."

"I'll tell you another tidbit. He insisted that there was a disgusting smell. Did you smell anything?"

"Not me."

"Me neither."

"More than madness, that's a total insult. How can there be a bad odor in this house where I break my back to keep everything clean?"

Fernanda, the one from 5B, came in from the street with the triplets and the twins. She was young, blonde, and divorced. She greeted Clotilde and went up in the elevator. "How unlucky I am," thought Ravenna. "I don't exist for the woman I like."

"People are very strange," commented Doña Clotilde. "Just to think that Venancio, who ruined your night, is the same person who entertained children and adults when they served the hot chocolate at the twins' birthday party."

"Don't tell me that he also misbehaved in Señora Fernanda's house," asked Ravenna, who was barely listening and was ready to become indignant.

"Not in the least. For your information I should clarify that Venancio is a good person who has a heart of gold and plays the clown at children's parties."

Finally Ravenna could take the elevator. As it went by the sixth floor he noticed there was a nauseating smell. On the seventh he inspected the laundry room, but found nothing. He rushed into his apartment, ran to the bathroom, doused his face with an aftershave lotion. He reflected: "In the past I always had cologne on hand. A fine custom that we've lost." He said to himself that the perfume of the lotion did nothing; in any case he seemed impregnated with the horrible odor that there was in the upper part of the building. While he had that smell in his nose, it would not be possible for him to carry on a normal life. "6B was so right to think that the cause of the odor has to be in one of these apartments," he reconsidered. "My nose does not deceive me: there's a dead animal or the corpse of a human being around here somewhere. A murder? Perhaps because he suspected that, 6B insisted so much. No: he insisted simply because he couldn't stand the smell. I can't stand it either."

These considerations provoked in Professor Ravenna, who was basically a good person, a certain sympathy and some sense of regret toward 6B. He called the Borda Clinic and asked for Garay:

"Please, I beg you to let him go. I've discovered he's not crazy. In this house there is a filthy smell. I myself smell it."

Garay responded:

"You're taking a great weight off my back. Here he has not complained of any bad smell. I don't think he's any less sane than we are."

Led by an irrepressible impulse he ran to knock on the door of 6A. Señora Octavia, glittering in her sculpted satin dress, quickly appeared. Without losing his poise, Ravenna said:

"Can I come in?"

Perhaps because not enough time had passed since the episode with 6B, the lady replied:

"Some nerve."

"But I'm 7A, your neighbor."

Speaking with a pronounced movement of her lips, the lady asked:

"Could you explain to me what right that gives you?"

Turning her back on him, she looked up at the ceiling and exclaimed: "Not even if you were my lover."

As if the influence of those words started working in his head like the mechanism of a slot machine on the verge of spilling forth the prize, Ravenna reflected and reached a conclusion. He said:

"With all due respect, Madame, that's what I most desire in the world."

"You say what you feel and you're refined," the lady commented. "I like that attitude."

Ravenna saw that Señora Octavia's lips trembled, grew moist.

"Allow me," he said.

He kissed her, embraced her, began to undress her. She observed:

"It would be best to close the door," and as she repeated, moaning, "Not so fast, not so fast," she took him off to bed.

It didn't take long for Ravenna to get up and inspect the house. As he didn't find any dead animal, he threw a kiss to the lady and went off to continue his investigation. He rushed down the stairs to the fifth floor and knocked on the door marked with the letter A. There lived Doctor Hipólito Reiner, an ear, nose, and throat man. "Most appropriate, in these circumstances," Ravenna thought, a little in jest. The door opened.

"What brings you around these parts, Doctor?" asked Reiner. He wasn't young, his hair was unkempt, he had a vague look in his eyes and seemed weak.

Ravenna looked as if he were about to answer but said nothing, since he suddenly found himself devoid of the reason that led him to knock on the door. With disbelief, with joy, he noticed that the smell had, in effect, disappeared. He said the first thing that came to mind:

"I wanted to inform you that it's not impossible that some neighbor might appear and ask permission to enter your apartment, because of a nauseating smell."

Reiner declared that he didn't understand. With few changes Ravenna repeated what he had said, maintaining the reference to the nauseating smell.

"What are you insinuating?" asked Reiner, choked with indignation. "That my apartment is dirty?"

The difficulty of realistically explaining the facts tired Ravenna from the outset and very quickly exasperated him. He said:

"I'm not insinuating anything, but as I'm a little fed up, I'm going."

He was still on his way up to the seventh floor when he saw, through the grillwork door of the elevator, Señora Octavia coming down.

After hesitating a moment, he got out of the elevator and managed to follow the lady down the stairs. She had disappeared, however. "That was not enough time for her to get down to the ground floor," he thought. "She entered 5A or 5B." Overcome by curiosity, he waited at a bend on a landing. No sooner did he hear the elevator moving, or footsteps somewhere, than he would go down or up a few steps so as not to be caught spying. His movements reminded him of the comings and goings of a caged animal.

Octavia finally came out of 5A; upon seeing him, she exclaimed:

"If you still have that nasal discomfort, Doctor Reiner is your salvation. I'll confess to you that when you came to my house, I thought the whole thing was an excuse. But a while later I began to smell something. How horrendous."

"Does it still bother you?"

"Doctor Reiner cured me. He's a magician. You should see him."

"I'm cured. I was cured by spreading it to you."

"You were very bad, but now it doesn't matter, because Doctor Reiner cured me. He's a magician. He didn't give me any medicine. I thought that all he did the whole time was to auscultate me with his metal cornets. He looked inside my nose and examined every inch of my mouth."

"Why?"

"He should know, he's the magician. One visit was enough to cure me."

Ravenna said:

"Well, I'm off."

He went up to his apartment. He thought he should tidy up his school papers before they got lost in the disorder on his table. "I can't keep my eyes open," he murmured. He dropped into his chair, looked out the window at the blue of the sky, and when he made a gesture to pick up the papers he fell profoundly asleep.

He awoke refreshed. He went over to the window and beyond the infinity of uneven houses he saw a prodigious sunset. As if arriving at a conclusion, he thought that if he had Fernanda at hand, the one in 5B with the triplets and twins, he would convince her. Certain that the time to act had arrived, he ran downstairs. He met up with Fernanda—which he interpreted as a good omen—coming out of 5A—a less auspicious omen.

Without giving him time to react, Fernanda said:

"How lucky to find you."

"She's speaking to me for the first time," Ravenna thought, and answered:

"It's lucky for me too."

"I want you to congratulate me. I'm getting married to Hipólito. Doctor Reiner, you know. It's enough to make you die laughing. He came to me in a fit of despair over the bad odor, and a few minutes later we were madly in love."

He felt extremely tired, but managing to pull himself together to attempt a final defense, he argued:

"That smell is contagious."

"Don't tell me! It seems obvious that I brought the disease to the house. Now I must be immune."

This conversation was interrupted by the arrival of the elevator, with Doña Clotilde, who announced:

"Doctor Ravenna: Doctor Garay is waiting for you downstairs."

"I had forgotten," he exclaimed with dismay.

He said goodby, squared his shoulders, and went off to face his long weekend.

LOVE CONQUERED

"Tell me about it," he said.

I don't know quite how it begins nor where we are. When Virginia asks: "Do you remember what you promised?" I don't have the courage to tell her, once again, that next week we'll have lunch together, but that today my parents are expecting me. As if trying to avoid tension by confusing matters in a whirlwind of talk, I blurt out words. Probably through the association of ideas I speak about a restaurant opened in an old mansion last winter by a French cook named Pierre—in San Isidro? or San Fernando? Or did Pierre actually remain in the Southside? After some stuttering I vaguely remember the name and address—my slips of memory could suggest that to make myself seem important I was praising a restaurant I barely knew; and to show that I am a connoisseur I proceed to describe in detail the delicacies that they serve there—a description that perhaps seems out of place in a man of simple palate like myself. I'm trying not to invent some excuse out of cowardice or inertia, or to accept a compromise in order to save face. I am upset, I suppose, precisely because I've acted against my own will—to invent an excuse, not to accept any compromise.

As I don't manage to break free of Virginia, I then

have to find a way of letting my parents know that I will not have lunch with them. To make things worse my mother is already waiting for me in the Rosedale Gardens. I imagine her sitting on a bench, smiling and vivacious, as she is in a faded photograph taken of her some time ago in these same gardens and which now seems sad to me.

Going along the porch of our country house I reach the old study with its peeling plaster. It takes some effort to wake up my father, who is resting in a strangely crumpled position on the sofa. "I didn't sleep well last night," he says, to excuse himself. He's very happy to see me. Immediately I tell him: "I am not going to have lunch with you." My father doesn't understand at first, because he isn't completely awake, and I hurry to ask him to "let mama know." I want to leave before he rouses himself, because he is still happy and I know that very soon he will be sad.

I inflict that pain on them and on myself so as not to disappoint a woman for whom the date with me means (how to say it without being mean?) just that, a lunch date.

He gave me his interpretation:

"What this means is that you don't want to see them right now."

"We were such good friends," I said.

I didn't have the energy to explain.